The Power of the Crystalline Trees

BOOK 1 OF THE GOLDEN SPIRAL SERIES

g.c. Ramirez

Soluna Press
773 Jack Creek Road
Ennis, MT 59729 USA

www.goldenspiralseries.com

The Power of the Crystalline Trees/ g.c. Ramirez. —1st ed.
ISBN 978-0-9789273-1-8

DEDICATION

To my favorite Crystallines
Julian and Quincy

CONTENTS

INVOCATION FOR A LEADER

I have seen that the accepting of Crystalline Responsibility

is the equating of my mortal self with the power of wind and lightning

and of the morning dew

and of the seas and storms

and of the wolf song

and of stars and comets and of an autumn leaf

and of suns and solar winds.

It is the accepting of my Crystalline Power, my Cosmic Self.

Only thus may I live a Life that has caught the Essence, the Truth,

and will stand into eternity.

Only through total acceptance and surrender to the awesome scope of Crystalline Responsibility,

Only thus may I know that I have come to the Balance of All That Is

And it is me.

PROLOGUE

As the oldest living survivor in the forest before and after the Great Shift, I am the keeper of records and the great awakener of the seedlings. Forty-three rings have passed since the Great Shift. For the few remaining animal species, this has been a time of simple survival. For us, it has been a time of mastering our skills. Before the devastation of Earth during the Great Shift, was our Great Devastation by Humans. That was a time when we were at their mercy, cut down and destroyed by their greed, not their needs. Our vast communication networks were destroyed. Our living systems were broken. Then a hush descended on Earth, followed by tremendous shaking, winds and floods. For many, the Great Shift was the end. For us, it was the beginning. We woke to a new dawn on Earth, an essential creator of the Balance of All That Is. Now, those who align to us become our allies. Those who don't are eliminated from our midst. As the oldest living survivor in the forest before and after the Great Shift, I am the keeper of records and the great awakener of the seedlings.

I am the Mother Tree of the Forest of Dandaka.

CHAPTER ONE

THE MAP COMPASS

"Boy, come here." Boosha spoke from a dim corner of the room. The small shafts of light coming from under the door and around the shutters highlighted the dust motes barely moving in the air. The old woman on the simple handmade bed lay still, conserving her energy, but her quiet voice conveyed her usual power and authority.

Lan crouched awkwardly at the hearth, not quite comfortable with his recent growth spurt and lanky limbs. He stoked the fire while bringing the finishing touches to a pot of tea, hoping not to make a mess. Normally Boosha took care of this task, while he handled the gathering and chopping of wood. Being outside was always preferable to inside where he was prone to bump into and break things.

Standing up with a cup of tea in his hands, he lurched unevenly across the room toward Boosha's side, trying not to trip over his feet or hit the table.

"Boosha, let me get the doctor for you," Lan said, his voice strained. He set the tea down with a rattle on a little side table, managing not to spill any of it.

Boosha snorted. "Well, I might be close to dying, but he'd kill me for sure," she said.

Leaning forward, she grabbed his wrist urging him with her touch to listen to her message and not leave because of his fear.

"Take that," she said, pointing with her free hand at a leather rucksack leaning against the wall. He'd never seen it before.

"I'm sorry we've run out of time together," Boosha continued "There are things I still wanted to teach you and you haven't received your third initiation yet. You will have to get it from someone else. Don't worry, it will happen."

As he picked up the rucksack, Lan felt disoriented. What was Boosha talking about? What teachings and initiations was she referring to? He was completely confused by her message, but his concern for her divided his thoughts.

Lan tried to calm her. "You can tell me all this later, when you feel better."

"No, no, no!" she said. "This is the last chance we'll get. It must be now. You have been like a grandson to me, but I haven't told you everything. I thought I would have more time." Boosha struggled to sit upright.

Lan put his arm underneath her shoulders and helped her sit up, while wishing she would lie back down. He felt twisted inside. What did she want to say that was so urgent she overrode her own need to rest?

Boosha reached into the rucksack he was holding and pulled out an odd-looking object. "This is the most important," she said, handing it to him. It reminded him of long ago compasses that had stopped working during the Great Shift. Even if it could, the needle on this compass wouldn't point to one direction. As he looked at the face, he saw the needle make a wide arc across a green section, starting in the lower left corner that said Gavilan. He had no idea what that meant. The middle of the green area said Forest of Dandaka. This one he knew. He and Boosha lived right beside this great forest. The needle, stopping at the top right edge of the green section, said Asira. Each time he looked at it, Lan watched the needle sweep in its strange curve from the bottom left to the top right.

"You must follow the Map Compass as you would any map and it will take you to Asira," said Boosha.

Lan was so confused he wasn't even sure what to ask. "But why?" he finally managed to blurt out. He wanted to smack himself on the head. At the moment, that seemed the silliest question he could have asked.

Evidently Boosha agreed with him. "I don't have time to explain it all to you." Boosha cut him off with a dismissive wave of her hand. "Just listen and remember what I am telling you right now."

Lan tried to bargain with her. "I'll go as soon as you feel better," he said.

"No!" Boosha exclaimed. "There are dark forces working to

change the Balance of All That Is and they must be stopped before the world shifts beyond the tipping point again. We were going to go together to Asira but now The Gatherers are coming. You must leave before they get here or they will take you as they did...." Her voice trailed off and then she muttered, "others."

Lan winced. He knew what she had been about to say. She'd almost said his parents. He was too young to remember when The Gatherers had swept through their village and taken his mother and father, essentially turning him into an orphan. Usually they just snatched up the children with the piercing blue eyes. But that time was different.

Where they took the children and his parents, or even if they were still alive, remained a mystery. After his parents vanished, Boosha had taken him under her wing and raised him as her own. Through the years, Lan had tried to get Boosha to tell him more about what happened to his parents, but she never answered and left it to him to decide their fate.

"All right," he surrendered, nodding sadly. Everything was moving too fast for him to take in, but he knew that the quiet life he'd lived was over and something new was beginning.

"Tell me what to do."

Boosha stopped to catch her breath, and Lan handed her the tea he'd made from willow bark. She nodded her head in thanks and acknowledgement, and stared intently at Lan. It made him nervous. He felt like she was sizing him up for something, but he wasn't sure for what. He must have passed the test because Boosha reached into the rucksack and handed Lan the next item.

"When you arrive at your destination, you must wear this" she said and handed him a deep blue cloak trimmed in gold and made with the softest of wool fibers. Geometric shapes were embroidered throughout the fabric.

Lan felt his face flush hot. "No way!" he said, rebelling at the thought of it. He had no idea what this task might be that she expected him to complete, but he knew it was NOT going to involve putting on an attention-grabbing cloak!

Everyone in the village wore the same simple, functional clothing. His sandy-colored tunic and pants were completely comfortable against his skin while not restricting his movements. More than fitting in with the village, though, he felt his clothes matched who he was… someone who could disappear at the back of a crowd or in the fields around the village. He'd spent a good deal of his life not drawing attention to himself. He wasn't going to start now with an expensive-looking cloak.

"Boy!" Boosha barked. "We have very little time left. I can't explain everything right now. You must listen to me and do exactly as I tell you."

Reaching into the bag, she pulled out the last item: a large crystal in the shape of a cube. She placed it in Lan's hand. At first it felt cold and heavy, then a warm, iridescent light shot out of its center, startling him in the dim room. It only lasted a few seconds, but if he bent over and looked into its core, he could still see the swirl of the light. He couldn't take his eyes off the mesmerizing movement of colors.

"You must take this to Asira," she said. "And deliver it with the Three Keys." Boosha placed her hand over the crystal cube, demanding that he look up at her. "Its name is Empowerment," she whispered. "Protect it and keep its name secret."

Lan's eyes widened and he stared at Boosha like an animal looking at a hunter. He could barely get himself dressed and out the door without tripping or breaking something. He was never on time, often losing himself in the frisky movements of a dog chasing a stick, or children running through the village center, playing tag and shouting with laughter. He had been told many times by other villagers he was not dependable. Lan liked that no one expected very much from him. A low bar from others meant he wouldn't be asked to do things that he might mess up.

Lan knew he was going to irritate Boosha again, but he couldn't stop his racing thoughts tumbling from his head into the space between them. "But who do I give it to? And why am I giving it to them? Will they know what it's all about? What if they ask me for more information? What if I give it to the wrong person? How long is this going to take?"

Then rising from the depth of his being, Lan admitted in anguish, "I can't do it. Don't ask me."

Boosha held up a finger to shush him. "Listen!" she said. "They are coming. You must leave immediately. Go out the back door and into the forest. They won't follow you there. Be quiet and don't make any noise. No matter what happens don't come back until you've delivered Empowerment to Asira. Follow the Map Compass and it will take you through the forest."

"But who's going to take care of you?" Lan asked, not ready to leave her yet. He was acutely aware that up until now his own survival depended on Boosha, even during her illness when she'd become dependent on him. Though she wasn't actually a relative, Boosha was the only family he had. He clutched the edge of her blanket with tight fists.

"I'll be fine," Boosha replied. "I'll be here when you get back. Now go! They're coming!"

When she spoke in that commanding voice, Lan knew to never cross her. He grabbed the pack and the belt that held his simple wilderness gear off the hook by the front door and raced out the back door. He heard shouts and banging off to his left. Crouching low while still trying to run as fast as he could, he crossed the small field between the village and the forest. The dry corn stalks, left over from harvest a few weeks earlier, threatened to trip him while shouting out his location with their treacherous rustling.

Lan's heart pounded in his ears and he fought to control his ragged gasps. His mind lurched and he felt the Earth tilt, threatening to rise up and smack him in the face. Behind him he could hear the sounds of marching and cries of fear from the people in the village. He imagined The Gatherers tearing through each house.

He reached the edge of the forest without anyone seeing him and stumbled into the cool darkness, nearly falling head first when his legs stopped. It was hushed and still, not just the absence of sound but of some living presence, aware and watching. Even underneath the dim forest canopy, a sparkling quality of light emanated from the trunks and leaves. His panic began to fade. He always felt at home in this forest.

Stepping behind a huge tree with lots of branches, he fought to control his breath and calm his mind. His first thought was of his own safety. Then he flushed with shame. What in the world was he thinking, leaving Boosha in her time of greatest need? He had reacted so immediately to her command, he hadn't given one thought to her well-being. Behind him came more shouts and cries of concern. What were The Gatherers doing to Boosha? He felt agony at the thought of them harming her. He couldn't continue one more step without knowing she was safe.

Lan climbed the tree, the rough bark scraping his hands. He moved cautiously to not create any movement in the branches that could be seen by others. He finally reached a spot high enough to allow him to look back at the village but still hide behind the dark jade leaves. Their soft, quiet touch on his face seemed surreal against the scene in the village. Several of the cottages were burning. People were running in total chaos trying to get away from The Gatherers. His heart lurched in his chest as cries, shouts and the yelps of dogs carried across the field. A group of large men in red and gold leather uniforms dragged Boosha by her hair into the square.

"Where is he?" they shouted at Boosha. She crossed her arms over her chest and didn't speak. The Gatherers scanned the crowd, obviously looking for someone.

"Boy!" they shouted. "If you want to save this old woman, you better get out here right now!"

Lan felt his stomach quiver but held himself absolutely still. Were they yelling at him? He couldn't let them do anything to Boosha. He started to climb down the tree but stopped when he felt Boosha glaring across the village and the field, through the leaves and right into his eyes.

"Don't you dare move. Do as I have told you." He heard her words inside his head as if she'd spoken them to his face. His mind raced erratically, not understanding how this was happening. Could she really see him? He instinctively shifted deeper into the tree, afraid that others could see him as well.

Clinging to the branch and barely breathing, Lan watched as The Gatherers continued to ransack the village. They seemed determined to find someone, but Lan still doubted all this was just for him. He was nobody, invisible to most of the villagers. They saw him only as the boy who helped the old woman, fetched her wood and got her herbs.

Now Boosha, on the other hand, was someone of importance in the village. She used her knowledge of plants to help people heal from wounds and illness. She was also known for her skills in predicting the future, especially the weather. The farmers depended on her for advice on when to plant, harvest or protect their fields. Weirdly, people also sometimes asked Boosha about their affairs of the heart. They made her chuckle. Under the guise of a potion to make someone fall in love, Boosha would dispense wisdom about what a loving relationship really entailed. She showed people how to love themselves first and open their hearts to be in a relationship.

Lan always watched in amazement when she helped the villagers. She had endless depths of insight that she dispensed with ease and confidence. He wondered where it came from. He felt completely blank inside about the life challenges that people brought to her. He couldn't imagine giving advice to anyone.

To him, Boosha seemed to be a part of everything while he didn't feel connected to anything. He liked her telling him what to do and organizing his day for him, because he had no idea what he would do otherwise. Once in a while, he had wondered what would happen to him when he was older and Boosha was no longer around. He mostly dismissed those thoughts because that time was surely years down the road. Now, for the first time, he began to realize how wrong he'd been.

Lan snapped back to the present. His hands clenched a branch so hard his knuckles had turned white. Little broken twigs poked into his hands leaving dents. He shook out his hands, knowing he needed to move deeper into the forest, past the place he and Boosha visited regularly to search for mushrooms and other plants.

He wasn't fearful about being in the forest, but he knew most other people were. Many had entered the great Forest of Dandaka but never came out again.

But he couldn't leave before knowing that Boosha was safe. Tossed aside in the village clearing, she was lying completely still. Not tearing his eyes off her, Lan didn't notice that The Gatherers had begun searching behind the houses. Suddenly one of them shouted. All eyes turned toward the loud voice, including Lan. The Gatherer standing behind his house had found the trail Lan had left through the broken corn stalks. An angry group of The Gatherers began racing across the field, straight toward the edge of the forest.

Lan's heart went into overdrive, knowing he had just a few minutes before they discovered him. Lan stared at Boosha, needing to know she was safe before he could leave. Wiping the sweat and tears from his eyes, Lan saw Boosha's hand move. He realized she was waving to him to go. His breath exhaled sharply. She was tougher than she looked. She'd be all right.

Released from his frozen stance, Lan fell out of the tree with a thud. It wasn't graceful, but it was certainly the quickest way down. He grabbed his rucksack and began to run deeper into the forest. He tried to keep quiet, but as he gasped with exertion and fear, sobs erupted from deep within him. His legs pumped harder and harder as he occasionally turned frantically to look behind him. Gradually the bright light at the edge of the forest grew smaller as he ran deeper into the muted interior. The sounds of his pursuers faded away but he still continued to run headlong into the forest.

Overcome by the terror and shock of the past couple of hours, Lan didn't notice the tangle of roots. His foot caught and he crashed to the ground, the wind knocked out of him. For a moment, he lay there, completely disoriented. All of his known reference points for his life were gone. His confusion wasn't so much The Gatherers chasing him as the strange information Boosha had dumped on him in the last few seconds with her. It made no sense. No sense at all.

Lying on the bumpy roots that stretched out from the base of the tree, Lan tried to catch up to what had just happened. He fought to recover his breath as well as his sense of the world. One thing was clear—he couldn't run one more step and needed to find a place to hide. Three roots that crisscrossed each other made a small enclosure. Lan wedged himself underneath the roots with his back toward the tree and his view toward the forest. From here he'd could hide from anyone crazy enough to follow him into the forest. Besides providing good cover, the roots felt like arms hugging him, which he definitely needed right now.

Although his body had stopped moving, Lan's mind raced as he replayed the past couple of hours for clues that might help him cope with his current predicament. Gradually his hot and sweaty face cooled down and he smelled the aromatic wood of the roots and pungent mustiness of dirt.

A sudden memory popped into Lan's mind of the last time Boosha had brought him to the forest. She was looking for a certain kind of herb that helped people with bunions. Lan wasn't the least bit interested in helping her. He had been busy tracking a butterfly as it floated through the undergrowth. Its bright luminescent greens and blues seemed to attract a ray of sunshine that had escaped the leafy canopy overhead and reached all the way to the muted browns of the undergrowth. Lan was hoping he could somehow talk the butterfly into landing on his hand. Boosha called those his foolish notions.

Now in his miniature root cave, Lan fought to remember what she had been telling him as he watched the butterfly dip its tongue into the nectar of a flower. He was so close he saw the tongue, more like a straw, curl back up in a spiral. Boosha was saying something about how important it was to take care of your feet, in case you had to walk or run for a long period of time. Was she trying to warn him about this time? he wondered.

At the memory of his beloved Boosha, sobs once again spilled out of his throat. Tears streaked down his cheeks and puddled in his ears. Would he ever see her again? Up until today, The Gatherers had just been shadowy figures like the stories of the boogey men under a kid's bed. They didn't seem real, but who wanted to find out for sure?

Lan racked his brain for memories. Had Boosha ever said something about The Gatherers coming back for him? He remembered the village celebrating the end of a long work week by sharing stories and songs around a communal fire. As the younger children began to fall asleep, the elders talked in hushed tones about darker things in the world.

Mostly the stories were rumors about The Gatherers coming to some village or town near them and how they took certain children and then destroyed the villages as they left. It was a strong message to others not to get in their way, nor to be foolish enough to follow them.

Lan's village consisted of just a handful of huts housing a few families. They lived simply with the land and the seasons. The villagers knew there was nothing of interest to anyone in their village, and they felt safe in that sense of anonymity. "Don't stand out and you won't attract trouble," was an unspoken motto in the village. Maybe that's why their town didn't even have a name.

The Gatherers always wanted the children with the piercing blue eyes. It was rumored those children could see in the dark like cats. The children of Lan's village, though, only had brown eyes so they and their parents felt safe from the raiders. Lan himself had what he called boring brown eyes.

There was always a moment in the storytelling when the villagers remembered the one time The Gatherers had come for someone other than children and they would stop talking and look uneasily at Lan. He thought they were looking at him because they took his parents. But now, crammed into his hiding spot, he wondered if they stared at him for another reason. Did they know The Gatherers would come back for him one day?

Lan suddenly felt trapped by the roots instead of held safely. He struggled to escape from his little cave, then gave up and sank back into the roots' embrace. Had everyone known these things but him? If Boosha knew, why hadn't she told him anything, or at least warned him? He remembered her saying something maybe a month ago about planning to go somewhere together. Then Boosha had fallen ill and for more than three weeks she'd been in bed with fevers and a cough that wouldn't go away.

That was a scary time for Lan. During those weeks, he'd had to forage for food and then prepare it, hoping not only that it would be appealing to Boosha but also nourishing. He tried to remember exactly how Boosha had made the different soups and broths for him. Their food was simple fare made from grains, mushrooms, and greens, but always savory. He would use the same ingredients but somehow the result didn't taste as good as hers. Half the time he was afraid he'd make something that would kill her instead of nourish her. Every now and then a neighbor would bring a dish over to them, for which he was grateful. Even though Boosha wasn't eating much, at least he knew she was getting a nourishing meal once in a while.

As sick as she was, Boosha had still known The Gatherers were coming. How was that possible? Lan wondered. When had she prepared his rucksack and where did she get those strange things she'd given him? He knew every inch of their small home and he'd never seen any of those items, nor the bag.

Lan squirmed under the roots to avoid the one poking him in the back while his thoughts struggled away from the task Boosha had given him. He felt despair to the depth of his being. If he'd missed so much of what was going on around him, how was he going to do what Boosha asked him to do? He had no idea how to take care of himself in the woods, how long it would take to get wherever he was supposed to go, or even what he was supposed to do when he got there. Handing someone a crystal cube named Empowerment seemed fairly straight-forward, if he knew who to give it to. But what about those three keys he was supposed to deliver? He didn't have any keys.

Lan heard a low moan and realized it came from deep in his chest. He was beyond caring if he was heard or discovered. Getting captured seemed a better alternative than facing this present moment alone. His mind raced over the task Boosha had given him to do. First, he was going to have to cross the great Forest of Dandaka alone. The same forest that swallowed people up forever. If he managed to do that, he was going to have to deliver random objects to people he didn't know for reasons he wasn't told, in a gaudy blue cloak. Every fiber of his being shrieked against the thought. He shrunk as small as he could under the roots, not caring if he was poked in the back or not.

He began whispering, "I can't do it, don't ask me. I can't do it, don't ask me. I can't do it, don't ask me."

The dim daylight slowly faded in the forest and became the blessing of darkness. Overwhelmed and exhausted with the events that had just turned his life upside down, Lan fell into a dreamless sleep. Mercifully, he stopped thinking and feeling.

CHAPTER TWO

LOST

Whack! Something hit him on the head. Whack! It happened again. Startled from his deep sleep, Lan tried to sit up. He immediately cracked his head on the roots. For a moment he couldn't figure out where he was. Why wasn't he in his comfortable bed back home? Hearing chattering above him, Lan looked up and saw a squirrel dropping nuts.

"Hey!" Lan yelled at the squirrel, and it scampered off to another branch. Evidently he'd been lying in the squirrel's treasure trove judging by the raucous chattering erupting from the branch overhead.

Yesterday's events came flooding back and Lan slowly climbed out from among the roots. His body hurt. His mind felt dull and his mouth had a foul taste. Boosha called his morning moods "getting up on the wrong side of the bed." Lan grunted. This was more like getting up on the wrong side of the roots.

He was parched, his eyes gritty and his throat raw. For a moment all his new challenges receded as the need for water outweighed all other concerns. He began searching for Water Plants.

Boosha had taught him how Water Plants grew around the bases of the mammoth trees and helped each other. The trees fed the Water Plants sugars through their roots, and the plants released collected water into the roots of the trees. It was a simple mechanism that solved a way to get rain past the leafy canopy of the big trees.

As the night air cooled, water droplets formed on the leaves. Folding into themselves at night, the leaves prevented the water from escaping. When the air began to warm during the day, the leaves opened and the collected water trickled out. Lan loved watching when they began to open their leaves. For a brief moment, it sounded like the tinkling of a wind chime as they released their tiny water bundles. Before he knew the real story about Water Plants, Boosha had told him it was the fairies shaking out their wings after the night dew. Knowing the truth hadn't taken away the magic of these plants.

Two trees away from his root bed, Lan spotted a dozen or so bright emerald Water Plants with their leaves still closed. He bent down and placed his lips close to the end of the leaf and then drank the tiny teaspoon of water. Although it barely made it to the back of his throat, it was incredibly refreshing. If anyone ever asked him what the color green tasted like, he'd tell them to drink this water.

Lan worked his way around the base of the tree through all of the plants. Slowly he began to replenish the water in his body. It took him almost 20 minutes before he felt satiated. He used the water from the last several leaves to wet the tail of his shirt and then wiped his face. Lan was sure he had tear streaks down his cheeks which he wasn't feeling too proud of today.

As he straightened up from the plants his stomach rumbled, telling him he'd need to look for food soon. His overriding desire to just finish the task Boosha gave him made him push the hunger to the back of his mind. He opened the rucksack and pulled out the Map Compass. It showed the same two points as before and the sweep of the needle through the Forest of Dandaka. It also had a new point on it which Lan figured must indicate his current location.

Lan took out the crystal cube and turned it over in his hand, wondering what was so important about it that he had to carry it such a long way. For a moment he stared into its center, fascinated with the swirl of iridescent light, then shook himself out of the beginning of a dreamy phase. He couldn't afford to lose track of time or his location by zoning out. Lan put the crystal back under the soft, flashy cloak, which he tried to ignore. If it turned cold at night, he might use it as a pillow or a blanket, but only if no one was watching.

His misery and fear for Boosha, and the memory of the raid by The Gatherers yesterday rose up into his throat and made his jaw ache with longing for her and their life. The sadness made him lash out in anger. With every fiber of his being he didn't want to do this task he'd been given. He started stomping on the Water Plants, yelling, "I can't do it! Don't ask me!"

Stopping to catch his breath, he suddenly realized what he had done to his favorite plants. He was relieved to see he hadn't actually broken any stems. A few were already popping back up. What was wrong with him? Where was his honor? Boosha wanted him to go to this village called Asira because she couldn't do it. He got that. And he'd do anything for her, especially if it would help her get well. His heart softened. He wouldn't go back to Boosha until he'd delivered the crystal. He envisioned the villagers clapping and cheering him as he strode back triumphantly into Boosha's waiting arms.

A smile on his face with the vision of "All hail the returning hero," Lan decided to think outside of the...cube. His mind flashing with the colors of the crystal, Lan muttered under his breath, "I mean, really, how long could it take anyway?"

For starters, why did he have to follow the curved path of the Map Compass? That was just going to add extra miles he didn't need. What if he just walked in a straight line to the point that indicated Asira? He was pretty good at orienting himself to the sun and he had the Map Compass as a backup. He'd worry about what to do when he got to the village later. For now, he had the beginning of a plan and a way to proceed that suited him just fine. Anytime he could accomplish something a different way, smarter than the original idea, he'd find himself smirking. When Boosha saw that look, she'd say, "Uh oh, here comes trouble." But she often applauded him for his creative thinking.

Lan began to tune in to his surroundings. Although it was dimmer under the trees then out in the fields, he could still see parts of the blue sky. He studied his shadow. It fell to his left, so he knew that was west. South was behind him and he wanted to head northeast. He changed his angle just a bit and started walking through the trees. He'd look for food as he went, eating what he could find without stopping to build a fire. In the far back of his mind, he wondered if he could build a fire without the help of Boosha or his friend John. He'd never done it by himself. He pushed the thought away. He'd worry about that when it was time to build one.

Lan felt like whistling with his new sense of confidence, but knew better than to make a lot of noise. He put his tantrum behind him hoping no one had heard him and, more importantly, that all the plants would recover.

Lan had never been in this part of the forest. Boosha usually stayed pretty close to the edge when she went foraging for plants. She told him to never enter the forest if he wasn't invited. Lan wasn't sure what that meant. How would he know if he'd been invited or not? He snorted now at the thought of it. It was just another dumb idea that older people had that they never explained and that didn't make sense.

Lan inhaled deeply and his head filled with the delightful scent of a sassafras tree. He loved that tree. It smelled and tasted deliciously sweet in one of Boosha's teas. All the trapped misery in his chest fell away. He would not only take this journey and help Boosha, but all his other friends would think he was brilliant when he succeeded!

Up ahead ran a small, quiet brook. Lan unhooked the copper cup from his belt and looked for a quiet pool to dip it in. Bending over, he grimaced when he caught sight of his reflection. His straight, brown hair was sticking up in several places, with a few leaves stuck in it. Self-consciously he raked his fingers through his hair, glad no one had seen him like that. His eyes, which he'd always described as boring brown, were red and swollen. He couldn't do anything about that or the smattering of freckles across his nose and the rounded, smooth cheeks lingering from his childhood. He'd heard two girls giggling once about his cute baby looks, but that just made him dislike his looks even more. At the moment, he was glad no one else was in the Forest of Dandaka.

Lan dipped his cup into the water, breaking up his image. Drinking deeply, he flipped the last few drops from the cup into the air. They caught the sunlight before falling to the bright green moss under his feet. Stepping lightly on the rocks to avoid slipping, Lan crossed the small stream. A sudden movement of air just over his head startled him and he looked up to see a small hawk land on a branch in front of him. It stared at him intently. How odd that it was hunting in the forest and not out in the field. The hawk's sharp, glittering eyes focused on him and gave him an unsettled feeling for a moment. Then Lan caught sight of a blackberry bush with some berries still on it below the hawk's perch. Not caring about his table manners, Lan rushed over and grabbed and stuffed as many as he could into his mouth. He knew they wouldn't fill him up completely, but the berries might give his stomach something to do other than rumble loudly. He'd keep a sharp watch for more food as he continued.

Lying on the ground in front of him he discovered a perfectly straight stick an inch thick and just about as long as his arm. With a little bit of carving, it would be ideal for digging roots or making fire pits. He picked it up and tucked it in his belt. When he stopped for the night, he'd prepare the point as John, the carpenter, had shown him. He went back to silent whistling as he strode off again. This was going to be easy!

Lan continued to travel with a bounce in his step through the forest, enjoying the day. He refused to let himself worry about Boosha. She'd be in the village waiting for him after his adventure and they'd have a laugh about things, like the squirrel scolding him. His life would go back to the way it had been.

His shadow had switched from the left side of his body to almost nothing, then began showing up on his right side. It was past noon when he approached a thick grove of willows that ran east to west as far as he could see. Stopping to admire the silver leaves against the reddish branches, Lan remembered all the times he'd cut willow branches for Boosha. She used the leaves for tea to ease pain and the branches to make baskets. Lan loved that in the Balance of All That Is, willows wove together the edges of a stream bed to prevent erosion while they were also great for weaving into furniture.

Just before Lan's life had turned upside down, John had promised to show him how to make a bent-willow chair. He didn't know if the willows would still be pliable by the time he got back. The thought, "if he got back" trickled through his mind, but he pushed it away. He couldn't...no, wouldn't, think like that right now.

Keeping to his plan to make as much progress through the woods as possible, Lan decided to cut through the willows instead of hiking around. The willows bunched tightly together from the ground to their waving tips above his head. They did an effective job of keeping out larger animals that might chew on their soft inner bark. Lan wasn't exactly small or short, but if he was careful where he placed his feet, his long arms could push back the willows to make room for the rest of his body. Stepping into the willow forest and opening the branches in front of him, Lan felt more than up to the task. A little bit of tough navigating in exchange for a shorter path was a good trade off.

Lan's good mood began to slip just a bit as he maneuvered through the willows. Their pungent, almost minty, smell seemed to be getting stronger as he resorted to twisting and turning and squeezing through the branches.

He began to get irritated with his slow progress. Was that just his imagination that the trees were getting harder to get through? He'd push several willow branches aside and they pushed back! They grabbed Lan's tunic and threaten to tear the fabric if he moved too fast. He had to be careful with his clothes. They were the only ones he had. Who knew how long they had to last.

Lan's appreciation for willows and all the ways they helped him in the past turned to resentment as they blocked his path. Like trying to break through a line of people with linked arms, the task felt impossible. It was one of him against the many willows. The only thing that kept him going was the determination not to turn around and go back. That would mean losing a whole day on his journey, not to mention having to admit to himself he'd been wrong with his plan.

Now a new misery presented itself. Small black flies began attacking him, attracted to his sweaty neck and hands. The first bite felt like it took a chunk of skin from under his ear. Without thinking, Lan released the willow branch he was holding to slap at the fly. The branch immediately smacked him in the face, leaving a welt. It was clear he was going to have to just let the flies bite him until he forced his way out of the willows.

Lan was so intent on moving forward, step by grueling step as he fought and wrestled with the willows, that he failed to notice he'd reached the end of the stand. Like being launched from a sling-shot, the willows ejected him from their midst. He almost sailed off the cliff in front of him. Gasping from exertion, Lan scrambled back from the edge.

Before him lay a rocky ravine filled with piles of jagged, black shale. Breaking up the rocks were dark, leafless trees. It took him a moment to realize that what he thought were tree branches were actually up-ended roots. Like frozen mouths they gasped for earth instead of air. Everything was a shade of black, including the tree trunks, the rocky shale, and even the dark stream at the bottom. The sunlight, incapable of penetrating the ravine, had been sucked out of every object.

Lan's heart sank. This was a sizable challenge to navigate that made the willows seem easy in comparison. He was going to have to climb over a lot of dead timber on slippery footing on the way down and then do the same climbing back up the other side.

Sitting down with the ravine in front of him and the willows to his back, Lan plotted out his route. He could see that the other side of the ravine offered only a few places where he'd be able to climb out. He had to get his navigation points clearly in his mind before starting. He imagined Boosha giving him a nod of approval for not launching himself headlong down the gully.

Apart from the need to make a plan, though, he was glad to catch his breath. His hair was sweat-plastered to his head and neck. It was going to dry in stiff, hard clumps. He hated when it looked and felt like that. The fly bites were starting to burn and swell from the sweat and heat of his skin.

One good thing about willows was that they grew in moist areas. Reaching into the rotted debris at the base of the willows behind him, he dug into the moist dirt and decomposed willow leaves and began applying the mixture to his neck and then hands. He put some on his face, too, where the willow had smacked him. The mud compound was cooling and he felt instant relief. The flies stopped swarming around his head now that they couldn't reach any bare skin. The relief was so great he didn't care what he looked like with his bright red face, plastered-down hair and muddy neck and cheeks.

While he contemplated a way through the tree maze and the ravine, Lan picked up the stick he'd found. Taking the knife from his belt, he carefully notched the end, making a point on one side but leaving the other side untouched. John had explained to him that one notch kept the digging end strong while two notches would weaken it.

And just like that he had his digging stick. He immediately dug a hole between the willows, knowing it would fill up with water to drink. When the water reached close to half a finger, he carefully dipped his cup into it. He rolled each mouthful around his tongue and inside his cheeks before swallowing. It didn't taste as crystal clear as the liquid from the Water Plants, but his body was grateful for hydration.

After all the exertion to get through the willows, Lan not only felt ravenous but also a bit weak. He hoped he'd find some mushrooms on the dead trees below and failing that, some kind of insects that he could eat. He flinched at the thought of having to munch on bugs but his stomach was driving the need for food and it wasn't being particular about the type.

Lan peered intently at the ravine in front of him and spotted a fallen tree off to his right that crossed the creek. He'd have to angle that way on his way down. He noticed a good spot off to his left on the other side for making his way out of the ravine.

How could he keep his bearings once he was in the darkness of the ravine? What he needed was a marker to help his navigation. Lan spotted several light-colored stones near him and began stacking them on top of each other to create a pyramid. They weren't perfectly white, but they were lighter than the rocks in the ravine and stood out against the backdrop of the red willows. His simple pyramid would direct him to the right angle to reach the log bridge, then he could reposition himself to reach the spot for climbing out on the other side.

Lan drank one more cup of water and stripped some leaves off the willows to take with him. If the bug bites continued to bother him, he'd have a remedy on hand. Then he lowered himself cautiously over the edge. Immediately his feet sank into the loose shale and he began to slide, arms flailing to keep his balance. He managed to stay upright until he reached the first log, but his momentum caused him to tumble over it. He landed face down, his hands breaking his fall, disturbing several rocks. Underneath ants were scurrying around trying to move their eggs to safety. His stomach over rid his squeamishness, and he began eating the round, white pellets that stood out starkly on the black rocks. Salty and crunchy, the eggs surprised him with how good they tasted. Lan wondered if it was because he was so hungry. He didn't know how many he'd have to eat to fill himself up, but it helped a little for now. Lan moved several more rocks looking for larvae while he was still on his stomach, then slowly got to his feet after he'd devoured them all.

Moving cautiously, Lan inched his way down the slope. Each step seemed to threaten a small avalanche or another fall. He had to decide whether to step between the rocks and risk slashing his ankles or step on the rock and have it shift and move. Slowly he began finding a rhythm. It wasn't graceful but it avoided face planting at each turn. Shifting sideways, he stepped down, waited for the rocks to quit moving, then stepped down again. When he arrived at a log, he skirted the huge roots until he reached a smaller part of the trunk. Climbing over it, he then started the step, stop, step down again.

Occasionally, he looked up to check his location in relation to the rock pyramid and then continued.

Lan was so focused on not falling he hadn't noticed the sounds coming from all around him till he stopped to rest his legs and knees. High pitched "eeeeks" came from certain rocks. He noticed small clumps of cut grass laying on the flat, sharp-edged stones, but Lan couldn't figure out what was making the sounds. Peering intently at one rock close to him, Lan finally saw a small, furry ball with big ears and no tail, hidden in the shadows of the rocks. It did not like the intrusion of the big giant in its backyard and warned the others about him. Lan had never seen one before, but Boosha had told him about these cute critters called pikas. Evidently this ravine wasn't as lifeless as it had appeared from above. That cheered him up and he felt slightly less alone.

It was getting late. The already dark ravine darkened even more. Lan decided to stop when he reached the bottom, where he'd have access to water and flat ground, then climb out first thing in the morning. Just then the hawk swooped over his head, crying out as it did. Startled, Lan stopped and looked up at the red flash of its belly as it sailed up the other side of the ravine and landed in a tree. It seemed to be the same raptor had he'd seen earlier. Was the bird following him? Lan shook his head, dismissing the thought as silly, but wishing he had his own pair of wings.

The pikas abruptly stopped calling to each other. Lan wondered if they were hiding from the sharp-eyed hawk. From above and off to his right Lan heard a low thundering sound. He turned toward the sound, trying to figure out what it might be. The sound grew louder, but Lan could not see anything making the noise. The willows were all stillness above him and the downed trees in the ravine had lost their ability to respond. Suddenly, he was knocked on his back as a savage, howling wind slammed into him. With the wind, total darkness descended.

Blinded and consumed by the howling wind, Lan crawled toward a large log, hoping to take cover. The wind buffeted him from over the top and around the sides of the trunk while roaring in his ears and sucking out his breath. Squeezing as tightly as he could into the rocks underneath the log, Lan curled into a small ball with his arms over his ears.

He'd heard of this wind and had been told it was a result of the Earth changes, but he'd never actually experienced it. People in the village said this wind could drive you mad. If this was what had knocked down the trees, how could he survive?

Throughout the night the wind relentlessly pounded him, blocking all of his senses. Lan was unable to escape it. He grew colder and began shivering. He briefly thought of retrieving the cloak from his bag but sitting up in the wind seemed impossible. And even if he succeeded in getting it, surely the cloak would instantly fly away or be shredded.

Eventually every thought was driven from his mind as he endured the endless onslaught of the wind. His eyes filled with so many tears they glued shut. When he tried to get a sense of time by looking at the stars, he discovered his eyes wouldn't open. Lan felt himself separate from himself. He became part of the landscape like one of the trees that had blown over. A pain in his head grew in crescendo to match the wind. He clung to one small point of light in his mind that was his last anchor to reality.

After an eternity of no-time, Lan slowly came back into himself. It was day. The wind had stopped. His ears throbbed in the deafening silence. He rubbed his eyes to unstick them but could barely see, they were so gummed up and gritty. It was strange to be in the ravine, now quiet in the daylight, as if nothing had happened.

Lan stood with legs trembling from cold and fatigue, and stumbled toward the swiftly moving creek. His whole sense of direction had been blown out of him during the night. Glancing back up at his rock pyramid, he was surprised and reassured to see it was still standing, glinting in the sunlight. Evidently the wind didn't stray out of the ravine. The sunlight at the top of the ravine woke a fierce longing to be out of this lifeless place. He sprinted across the log bridge and began making his way up the other side. It proved to be slow going, as he took a step and slid back, then took another step and slid back, but the hiking warmed him and his deep core shivering finally stopped.

Eventually he reached the top and felt a small flicker of relief that he'd navigated right to where he'd planned. With one final heave, he was out of the ravine. He lay on his back, looking up at the sky, exhausted, hungry and discouraged. He was beginning to doubt his plan and himself. A few more obstacles like the ones he'd just endured and he feared he'd be finished forever.

As the life force flowed back into his limbs, Lan's mood shifted. Maybe the worst was behind him. Lan chuckled, feeling his natural good humor restored now that he was safe. If only that wind had been in the willows, it could have done all the work of carving a path through the branches and kept the flies off him as well!

Up ahead, Lan caught a wonderful sight for his starving body. Could it be? Yes! A whole grove of pecan trees. Their grey, furrowed bark and towering sizes told him these trees had been around for a while. The last time he'd seen pecan trees this big, Boosha had told him they had to be at least 100 years old.

The ground was covered with hundreds of utterly delicious and nutritious nuts in their brown coverings. Eagerly scooping them up by the handful, he carried them over to the base of a tree that looked like a natural chair. Sitting down, Lan grabbed two rocks and began cracking the pecans open. Cramming the meat into his mouth, he kept eating until his stomach was full and extended. A satisfied belch was his signal to stop. Completely satiated, Lan rested in the sunshine between the trees. His limbs were so heavy he felt like he was melting into the ground. Listening to the bird songs in the grove, he decided to rest and take up his journey in a little while.

Feeling warm, safe and hopeful, Lan fell asleep with a smile on his face. He didn't see the hawk that swooped over him and disappeared into the tree branches, nor the fog that settled in, obscuring the sun. And he definitely didn't see the Map Compass go blank.

CHAPTER THREE

STARTING OVER

Lan woke with his face stuck to his arm, dried spittle acting as glue. He grimaced as he rubbed off the crusty stain on his face. The things his body did repulsed him sometimes. He never thought he'd miss brushing his teeth or changing his clothes, but the past few days had shown him how those simple actions helped him feel good overall. Now he felt gritty, grimy, and clammy. What had happened to the warmth from the sun?

His brain began to register the dense, grey fog that had settled in. The birds, twittering and singing in the pecan grove when he arrived, had gone silent. With no vision, his ears strained to figure out where he was. Getting slowly to his feet, he tried to peer ahead through the grove. At least, he thought he was looking the way ahead. With visibility less than an arm's length, nothing looked familiar. What if he walked in the wrong direction and plunged off the edge of the ravine? He'd have to either wait out the fog or proceed very slowly. Then Lan remembered the Map Compass.

Taking it out of his pack, he eagerly looked for the needle's sweeping arc and the point that would show his present location. The screen was blank. Thinking the moisture from the fog might be to blame, he wiped off the device. Nothing appeared. He shook it. It remained blank. Lan took a few steps in the direction he thought was right while watching the face of the Map Compass. Without even a flicker, it stayed maddeningly dead.

Should he wait out the fog until he could use the sun for guidance? Without the Map Compass, though, Lan's confidence in his plan was gone. Boosha always told him to stop doubting himself. What was it she said? If he received three positive signs, his inner knowing voice was telling him yes. But if he received three negative signs, that was a no. The trouble was trying to figure out if a sign was positive or negative. Like that hawk that swooped over his head twice yesterday, was that a positive sign? And besides, the bird hadn't appeared a third time so maybe that didn't count.

Just then a hawk's single sharp cry called out from somewhere in the fog, startling Lan with its timing. He guessed that could be the third sign, but was it good or bad? Lan thought back on the day before, looking for other signs, and began counting with his fingers. One! Those willows seemed like a clear "no." Two! That ravine and the awful wind, that had to be a "no." Three! The Map Compass going blank and the fog obscuring everything was certainly a negative sign.

Slowly it dawned on him. With the Map Compass going blank he wouldn't be able to proceed. If he wanted to avoid being lost forever in the Forest of Dandaka, he was going to have to follow his tracks back to where he'd started. Suddenly his heart lifted and he smiled. He could go back to Boosha and tell her he couldn't do what she wanted because the Map Compass had failed. He'd try to look upset when he told her.

Lan crawled under the trees, gathering pecans for the trip back. If he had any left, he'd even leave some for the squirrel in the root bed when he passed it by. Now, how to find his way to the ravine? Lan didn't think he was too far away but this dense fog could fool anyone's sense of direction and distance. He noticed it was slightly less foggy to his left and that's the direction he would have guessed for the ravine. He grabbed some rocks to mark his path. If he was wrong, he'd retrace his steps and try a new direction.

Moving slowly, Lan headed toward the lighter patch of fog. It didn't take him too long to reach the lip of the ravine. Only one try and he'd got it right! Already he was feeling like he was getting positive signs.

How strange the landscape looked. The fog stopped right at the edge, while the ravine was clear and so were the willows waving in the sun on the other side. Although he was grateful for the absence of fog, he felt gloomy thinking about traversing the ravine, remembering his first trip through it. He definitely was not looking forward to spending another night in that wind.

Sighing deeply, he told himself he just needed to get on with it. He'd already wasted enough time. If it took him as long to get back to the village as it took him to reach this point, he had a couple days' journey ahead of him, barring any more unexpected forest or weather challenges.

As his eyes searched for the rock pyramid he'd built on the other side to help with navigation, he suddenly became aware of a strange pattern with the fallen trees. A wild idea sprang into his head. Could he run down the trees, jumping from one trunk to another? He would be going very fast on the way down, and one misstep would be hazardous to the health of his limbs. He carefully traced the route with his eyes to the bottom. It looked possible. Lan then pretended to run the route, jogging in place and leaping from side to side as he ran down the trunks in his imagination. He had to jump to the right on the first one, then two lefts, another right, then left and he'd be at the bottom.

Pausing to catch his breath after his imaginary run, he looked at the other side. Could he run up those tree trunks? Out of the corner of his eye, he spotted a thin white path snaking through the shale. Tracing it to the top, Lan saw it took him to a gap in the willows which he hadn't seen before. He mentally marked its location in relation to the rock pyramid and then, without waiting any longer, launched himself off the edge onto the first trunk.

Flying down the steep incline, Lan kept an eye on the route, while letting his muscles remember when to jump. The trick was to keep moving before gravity could tumble him head over heels. It seemed like he had grown wings after all as he swooped down to the base of the ravine in minutes compared to the hours it had taken him before. He was laughing as he reached the bottom. For the first time in his life he got a glimpse of what it was like to move with grace and ease.

Amazed at how much time he'd just saved, Lan glanced back where he'd just come from. Taking a step, he immediately tripped over a rock and crashed painfully on his knee. He felt his pants tear and skin break. "Forctate!" Lan cursed. Boosha wouldn't have approved of his language, but she wasn't around, was she?

Lan looked for the trail he'd spotted from above. It started right across the creek. What looked like a path from above turned out to be drying grass laid out on rocks by the pikas. It was the light yellow against the black shale that had caught his attention. He followed the line up as far as he could see. It went right to the perfect exit spot.

Wondering if the drying grass would actually work as a trail, he leapt across the stream, wincing slightly when he landed on his leg with the bruised knee. Then he stepped onto the first grass-covered rock. It held firm beneath him. The pikas, however, erupted in a fury of high-pitched squeaks as they called out to each other in the ravine. Lan grinned. It seemed to be his fate to make small rodent creatures mad at him.

Continuing to step on each rock marked with grass, Lan moved smoothly and easily up the other side. Once he inadvertently kicked the grass off. He carefully picked it up and replaced it. Although the pikas didn't see him as a friend and wouldn't thank him, he was deeply grateful to them.

Once again, Lan reached the top in record time. What a difference from the day before. The light on this side of the ravine was beginning to fade and he hesitated before entering the willows.

He wouldn't want to run out of light in the middle of the thicket. He looked closely at the gap he'd spotted from the other side. About the width of one of his feet, it was narrow, with little pieces of grass all along the way. The pikas must have made this small trail to reach the meadow on the other side to harvest grass. It might just work for him, although he'd have to retrace his steps once through the willows to get back to his original path. He glanced at the rock pyramid to his left and measured roughly the distance from his present location. He'd use that measurement on the other side of the willows to return to where he first entered.

Placing one foot on the small path, his arms reached forward to push the willows back. This time, they parted easily almost the moment he touched them. How odd! Whereas before they seemed to impede his progress, now they seemed to open and let him through. Another sign that he'd made the right decision in turning around and going back

He walked through the willow stand quickly. Exiting, he turned to his left and followed the line of trees up to the point where he had first entered the stand. Now he could see his trail through the forest. The light was fading rapidly, though. He didn't want to lose the trail in the dark, so he decided to stop where he was and spend the night.

Other than the night in the ravine with the wind that had chilled him to the bone, the temperature during his first couple of nights had been fairly warm. Now it felt a little chillier. Lan decided to build a simple shelter by bending some willows and planting them in the ground. He'd watched one of the villagers make a willow structure for the kids to play in and he thought he could do it now, especially with his recent successes.

He began to strip back the leaves on a dozen strands of willow. Once he had enough, he took out his stick and dug 12 holes in a straight line, four fingers apart from each other. The plan was to weave other willow branches in and out of the supports but the supporting willows had a mind of their own. Some of them whipped out of their holes. Others leaned crazily to one side. Abandoning the idea of shelter, he decided that if he had a good fire, that would be enough.

Lan knew the steps to make a fire but had never built one of his own before. A little nervous about the whole process, he let his new confidence from the passage through the ravine and the willows quell his doubts.

He started with the fire pit. Using his digging stick, he cut a round circle in the grass then dug beneath it to break the roots. Peeling back the sod, he lifted it in one piece and set it aside. He'd replace it tomorrow, helping to put out any remaining coals and restore his campsite to the way it was before he stayed there. Smiling slightly, Lan knew John, who had shown him how to make fires in the wilderness and at home in the hearth, would approve of his fire pit.

Next he needed to make a tinder bundle that would catch the spark from his flint and steel. Keeping an eye on the remaining light of the day and never straying too far from his campsite, Lan began stripping off the inner bark from a fallen tree. He knew better than to wander from his original trail. In the ravine and even the forest, light would start to fade like a slight warning and then night swooped down like a heavy curtain dropped over a window. Under the forest canopy at night it was hard to see the back of your hand, much less stars or the moon.

Lan began rubbing the long tree fibers in his hands to shred them a little bit. Then he looped them around his fingers and tucked the end into the center, creating a little nest. Finding some lichen growing on the downed trunk, he tucked it into the center. He set it by his fire pit while he collected more twigs, then branches, then a good-size log or two.

Finally, he was ready to start his fire. Sitting where the doorway of his willow tent would have been, he took his fire kit out of his leather bag. It consisted of a small box that held char cloth. Already slightly burned, it started easily when a spark landed on it. He put the char on top of the spark rock he'd found last year. It had a nice flat surface to hold the char and a sharp edge to help create the spark when he struck it with his steel file. The file had been given to him by Sam, the blacksmith, from one of his that had broken.

Holding the spark rock in his left hand, he struck the file down the sharp edge. A spark flew off and careened wildly to the side. He struck the flint rock with the file again. The spark danced off the other way. Again and again he tried. With each miss, Lan's confidence dropped.

After several dozen tries, Lan gave up. Building a fire had always been what the adults had done. At 14, he'd felt grown up when he got his own fire kit. It seemed so easy to start a fire when John had showed him how. Now he just felt inadequate and helpless, all of his new-found confidence drained out.

As he gave up on his futile efforts to start the fire, Lan felt colder than ever. He decided to finally take out the colorful cloak. It slipped around him, warm and soft. He felt silly in it and still couldn't see himself wearing the fancy cloak in front of others. Imagining he'd arrived at the village, he swept up one edge and bowed deeply in front of an imaginary person. "Warrior Lan at your service," he said, clowning around. This little bit of playacting lifted his spirits and he chuckled.

Lan sat down in front of his unlit fire. He felt so good as the imaginary Warrior Lan, he decided to just imagine his fire was lit, too. His knee began to throb painfully. How typical...as soon as your attention was not on the immediate activity, your body reminded you of its bruises and aches. Stripping off some willow leaves, he chewed on them. They would have been better in a hot tea but they definitely eased the pain. It was easier to be grateful to the willows this time, since it had been so effortless to walk back through them.

Cracking pecans and munching on them in front of his imaginary fire, Lan reflected back on the events of the last several days and the one to come. What a difference it had been today compared with the first time he struggled through the forest, willows, and ravine. He'd been scared and hungry most of the time, then in a battle with the willows, and frozen and overwhelmed in the windy ravine. Other than the lack of success with building a fire and making shelter for the night, the journey back was like a beautiful summer day with white, puffy clouds overhead. Just the thought of heading back to the village made him feel more lighthearted.

Lan found himself shifting into his Deep Thoughts, as Boosha called them. When Lan was 10 he'd discovered he could take all the confusing things that were happening around him and swirl them deep into his belly. After a while, the soup of disjointed information would cook together and then the magic would happen. Rising from some place deep within that seemed like him, but not like him, a brilliant new insight would trickle up and burst inside his head. Sometimes he shared what he'd figured out with Boosha, who listened intently and nodded in affirmation, and sometimes he just kept his new understanding to himself. It embarrassed him to say it, but those moments he spent in his Deep Thoughts were holy and sacred.

This time as he began to sink into his Deep Thoughts, he felt inspired to take out the Crystal Cube. Even without a fire it seemed to catch light from somewhere and flashed out. Holding the cube in his hands, he followed his thoughts deep into his belly. Time passed as he sat like a stone. Suddenly energy released from deep within and traveled into his head. This time, though, the energy continued and he found himself out of his body. In that moment, Lan became Hawk with the sharply curved beak and piercing eyes that didn't miss anything. Through the hawk's eyes he watched himself when he was standing next to the Water Plants. The boy standing there was still angry about the journey he had been sent on. As the swift and powerful Hawk, Lan saw a shimmering grid of light that sank deep into the earth and rose into the sky. Everything was connected to it except the boy. Only aware of himself and his fear, Boy stood alone and miserable.

Effortlessly gliding along with his red feathers underneath and bluish-grey back, Hawk looked at the expansive Forest of Dandaka above while Boy struggled through the willows and tumbled down through the ravine. From the sky, Hawk watched as Boy ignored the signals that were obvious to the pikas. When the terrible wind blew, Hawk saw the Golden Grid disappear as everything that resisted was destroyed. Hawk wondered how Boy could survive, then swooped down and wrapped his soft feathery wings around him in protection.

As day broke, Hawk rose up and flew to the pecan trees. Perched on a branch he watched as Boy, full of pecans, laid down to sleep. Then the fog descended and obscured the Golden Grid, and Hawk knew the Map Compass had gone blank.

Lan's hawk vision continued as he sat in deep meditation. When Boy made the decision to go back the way he had come, he connected to the Golden Grid. Now Boy could see the natural staircase through the ravine, first through the fallen logs and then on the grass trail left by the pikas. When Boy paused in front of the willows, Hawk saw them nod and let him through easily. No wonder Boy knew they were helping this time instead of resisting him.

Hawk swooped down and merged into the back and head of Boy, who sat in front of his unlit fire. Still in an altered state, Lan reached down and grabbed his fire kit. He almost expected his arm to be a wing. He struck the steel file against the flint rock and a perfect spark flew up and landed dead center on the char cloth, catching hold. Without any hesitancy or doubt, Lan tipped the smoldering char cloth into his tinder bundle and blew on it. With a sudden whoosh, the bundle burst into flames, nearly singeing his eyebrows. He set it in the fire pit and began adding twigs, then bigger branches, until his fire burned brightly.

Lan looked around, still expecting to see the Golden Grid, but couldn't see it through his human eyes. Maybe it was due to the darkness. Curling on his side, Lan closed his eyes and slept with a smile on his face.

The next morning, Lan made some willow leaf tea in the remaining coals of his fire. He kept looking around for the Golden Grid but couldn't see it. As he replaced the grass plug where the fire pit had been, he pondered if the Golden Grid was something only a hawk could see because of its sharp vision, or if there was something he could do to be able to see it as well.

For now, his thoughts turned toward the village. He was excited that he'd get back home today. Walking quickly, he began retracing his steps. Even though he was approaching from the opposite direction, he saw several landmarks that he remembered passing the first time. He munched on pecans as he walked, humming softly to himself. Mindful of his self-made promise to leave a treat for the squirrel at the root bed, he didn't eat all of the nuts.

He crossed the stream where he'd first seen the hawk. Looking around, he wondered if it would be there to greet him. Lan still wasn't sure if the hawk was just a coincidence or a positive sign. He'd loved becoming the hawk during his Deep Thoughts. That was something he'd never done before.

As Lan approached the root bed where he'd spent his first night in the forest, he began to feel uneasy. He glanced up at the sky as a shadow came between him and the filtered light of the forest canopy. Above the leafy branches, all he saw was blue sky without a single cloud. Glancing around Lan couldn't see any logical reason to be tense, but he was feeling more anxious by the second. His steps slowed and he moved forward cautiously. The forest was still and hushed. Then he began to smell something, first faint and then stronger. It was a combination of rotting garbage, smelly socks, and something else he couldn't identify. He gagged with the overpowering smell.

Coming around a corner of a tree, Lan jumped and yelled in surprise before a hand clapped over his mouth. Two men in red and gold leather uniforms leered down at him triumphantly.

"We got you now!" exclaimed the one holding him by the arms. "You are going to pay for running away from us."

Lan's heart pounded in his ears. Desperately wanting to escape, he bit hard on the hand of the guard, drawing blood. The Gatherer swore and sharply pulled his hand away. "Why you little..." he exclaimed while the other Gatherer doubled over laughing at his pain.

"Draegan is going to love hearing how this kid with no skills or weapons drew blood from you," he snorted.

Lan swayed, suddenly dizzy. His nose became so stuffed he could barely breathe. The Gatherers started coughing violently and grabbing their throats. Using the moment of confusion, Lan stumbled away from The Gatherers, thinking they would pursue him but trying to get away nevertheless. Overcome with nausea Lan fell to his knees and began retching violently. Then everything went black.

Lan came to with his face pressed into some Water Plants. Their coolness felt good. He noticed he could breathe again then suddenly remembered The Gatherers. What had happened to them? Slowly getting up, Lan looked cautiously around. He could see a flash of red back by the root bed. Should he just continue to run away? He watched their still forms for a minute then cautiously walked toward them. Ready to run at the slightest movement, Lan tiptoed forward. As he got closer he smelled a whiff of something that caused him to gag again. Trying not to breathe the terrible stench through his nose, he wondered what had happened to them.

Convinced that they were either unconscious or dead, Lan walked up to them. He turned one of them over with his foot. The man's face was bloated and contorted, one hand grasping his throat. Bending down, Lan felt for a pulse on his neck, then recoiled with the stench. The smell, the same as the one in the air, was stronger and more pungent. Checking the second man, Lan couldn't discover any pulse either. Could that smell have killed them? If so, where had it come from? Lan remembered Boosha's warning about asking permission to enter the forest and how some people never came out again. Is that why he had survived and they hadn't?

Spooked by the whole scene, Lan backed away. He wasn't sure which was worse...almost being captured or the swift end of The Gatherers.

Moving away from the bodies while holding his hand over his nose, he stumbled over the root bed. The roots were destroyed—cut and hacked apart. The quietness with the taint of smell still in the air just heightened the absence of the squirrel. Feeling badly for the squirrel's mangled treasure trove, Lan reached into his rucksack for the last of the pecans. Maybe the squirrel would come back and find them. Groping for the pecans at the bottom of his bag, Lan took out the Map Compass and then stopped in astonishment. It was working again.

As if someone had hit him on the back of the knees, Lan sat down abruptly. Without the Map Compass being broken, he could no longer go back to the village and declare himself unable to complete the journey. The Gatherers were obviously still looking for him, even daring to search the Forest. Should he go back as he'd planned or start over from the right place on the Map Compass?

He felt the silent but familiar gliding over his head and looked right into the eyes of the hawk. Was that his imagination that the bird looked at him exactly the way Boosha did when she was waiting for him to make the right decision about something? Not knowing the answer, he decided to walk to the starting point on the Map Compass marked by the word Gavilan. He'd make up his mind when he got there.

Swinging his rucksack over his shoulder, Lan walked toward the beginning point on the Map Compass. Soon he was at the true start, just on the edge of the forest. As he pondered what to do next, he made sure to stay hidden in the shadows. He'd changed so much in the few short days since he'd begun this journey, it felt like a lifetime ago he'd run away from the village in terror.

Lan was in a beautiful spot in the forest that he'd never seen before. On one side, just a few trees stood between him and the fields that would lead back to the village. On the other side, a stream ran under a beautiful arched rock, then plunged over a small waterfall and into a pond. He felt himself pulled toward the crystal-clear water. At that moment, he spotted a bag leaning against a tree. Loping over to it, he discovered someone had left him food and clean clothes. Did Boosha do that, he wondered?

For now, all he could think of was tearing off his torn and smelly clothes and diving into the sparkling water of the pond. With a light heart, he raced down the stream bed, jumping from rock to rock. Giving a big "Whoop!" he jumped off the top of the waterfall and into the hidden depths of the water. Gasping with the coldness of it, Lan pulled himself out on a warm, flat rock.

As he lay in the sun recovering his warmth, Lan imagined himself going back to the village to find Boosha and all that was familiar waiting for him. Then he pictured himself moving through the unknown forest to the Asira point. He inhaled deeply then released his breath.

In that space between breaths, Lan knew exactly what he must do.

CHAPTER FOUR

THE VISION

Asira sat by the fire outside her simple hut. She felt curiously empty and flat, neither happy nor sad. This was the last night of her life. Beside her lay Takaani, the young wolf dog she'd rescued last year. Asira's hand stroked his beautiful soft head. One of the things Asira had had to do before she could do what she had planned was make arrangements for his care. Now all was in place and there was nothing to keep her here anymore.

Behind Asira were the muted sounds and sights of the town under the brilliant night sky. It was the time of the New Moons when their presence wasn't seen. The stars of the Milky Way highlighted the velvety void of the universe. The voices from town were an indistinct murmuring, and the light of other fires and lanterns flickered behind bushes and rocks. Although close by, Asira had the privacy she needed and wanted. She lived alone but seldom felt lonely. It had been like this for most of her life.

Asira grew up in a family who treated her kindly but weren't her real family. She didn't know what had happened to her parents and her adoptive family never told her. Asira felt so different from everyone she wasn't sure if her biological family would have made any difference in her life. She doubted it.

Her true family was made up of the animals all around her. She played with them, listened and responded to them with their picture language, and helped them when they were hurt. Sometimes they needed certain plants that they would show her through their picture words. Sometimes they needed stitching up from a wound. Asira could do it without hurting them as she threaded needle and gut through their skin.

When Asira was six or seven, she discovered she could just put her hands down on sick animals and they would start to get better. Her adoptive family never made a big deal out of her special gifts with animals. They always treated her as an equal and yet with an amused air, as though what she could do was normal for anyone her age.

Her gifts were not the norm, though, in the village. For as long as Asira could remember, others treated her with suspicion, sometimes cursing her or making threatening gestures for her to go away if she came too close.

Whenever something bad happened in her vicinity, she was blamed. If a couple were fighting and she walked by, they would turn on her and curse her for causing them to fight. Once the butcher sold spoiled meat to Kuut, the town director, and blamed her for causing the meat to go bad. Asira was even blamed for unusual weather such as a cold snap that froze the gardens before harvest.

The town was simply called "Our Place" by those who lived there. If it had a name that travelers from beyond the village used, Asira had never heard it. On one side of the village was a fast and wide river and beyond was the great Forest of Dandaka. On the other side rose a tall, grassy steppe and behind that a series of ever taller mountains that stayed white with snow most of the year. The travelers who came to their village often arrived from that direction.

The river between Our Place and the Forest of Dandaka was the mighty and powerful Urubamba. Those who knew how to navigate it used it to reach the town. To travel back, though, the boatmen had to hire great shaggy beasts, a cross between cow and bison. They pulled the boats back up the river.

Below the village, the river became even more wild and dangerous. It crashed through narrow canyons before spectacularly falling over a rocky lip for hundreds of feet. Asira had hiked to the top of the falls a couple of times. She loved listening to the powerful rumble of the water while her face and hair were gently misted. She spent long moments gazing into the green-yellow depths of the river, imagining herself floating peacefully over the edge into misty oblivion.

Asira's town was one of the few that hosted a wide variety of animals. It was the reason people from far away came to Our Place. They bartered for what they needed or wanted. Although they paid dearly to get there and then acquire an animal and return to their homes, the scarcity of animals in other regions automatically ensured a good return on their money.

Besides the shaggy cow-bison, Our Place was home to mountain ponies, donkeys, wolf-dogs, chickens, and cats. One spectacular bird, called the Firebird, was highly popular. Because of its brilliant plumage and haunting songs, it was prized more for an adornment than for its work service. The Firebirds were extremely difficult to trap and therefore the most valuable of all the animals.

All the creatures were either wild or half-wild. They roamed the countryside around the village. When the villagers needed a certain type of animal, they would corral it, use it for a little while, then release it. Chickens roamed throughout the streets and buildings and were encouraged to stay close with vegetable scraps. The children were in charge of watching their roosts at night and gathering the eggs in the morning.

Besides animals, the travelers from afar came for other wares. Near the village was a trash site that dated back before the Great Shift. It held all manner of items that were no longer found anywhere else and were highly useful. Glass containers in any form was eagerly sought after, although it was hard to find any that had not been broken. Plastic bottles that could hold liquid of any kind were also highly valued. Enterprising souls scavenged for different metals to make into lanterns or tools. Knives created from metal scraps were especially popular.

The townspeople would sift through the refuse site when they had time. They would use what they needed and stockpile the rest to sell to travelers when they came through. There was a loose agreement about the midden, as the villagers called the site. Anyone from the village could search for material to use or to sell, but the travelers who came through the village could not access it on their own.

The Gatherers in their red and gold uniforms were dreaded by everyone. Because they only took the children called the Crystallines, the villagers were hypervigilant about these children. If a baby with blue eyes was born in the village, either the whole family had to leave or the child was given to one of the travelers to take away. Most families chose to give up their children instead of enduring the uncertainty of living somewhere else. Asira didn't know what happened to these children when they were given to the travelers. She knew that over the years, though, fewer and fewer children with blue eyes were born.

Perhaps because the villagers were so terrified of The Gatherers, they thought Asira's strange healing gifts would attract their attention. They couldn't disqualify her from the village, though, because her eyes were brown. She had dark hair and skin to match. Since most of the villagers were fair-skinned and had light-colored hair, her coloring was one more reason she stood out. They thought her dirty because of her darker skin.

When Asira turned ten, things changed for her. Up until then, she'd helped her family each day with whatever chores they gave her. In her free time, she ran wild in the country around the town, climbing to the top of the steppe and looking for donkeys, mountain ponies or the cow-bison. She played and talked with them with their picture words. To her it was natural and easy and she couldn't figure out why no one else did it.

The animals showed her how they connected to the land and the stars overhead through a Golden Grid. They read the messages that were brought to them from the wind, the grasses, the water in the river and the clouds. Both animals and humans seemed to innately agree on the need to stay away from the Forest of Dandaka. Being naturally curious, Asira had wondered if it was the forest itself or the river they had to cross to get there. One day she found a way to cross the Urubamba River and she wandered into the forest. She didn't find the trees menacing or bad, just powerful. She wasn't sure if the trees distrusted her like most of the villagers did, or if they liked her as the animals did, so she was careful and respectful in the forest. After that one visit, she didn't return.

Then Asira turned ten, and she felt things shift inside of her. Her family had a little girl who was now four and followed Asira around the village. Susie was one of the few humans who Asira felt comfortable with. She didn't have to say much to her, but Susie loved babbling to Asira. The villagers were more tolerant toward her when Susie was with her.

Although on the surface things seemed to have gotten better for Asira, on the inside she felt worse. When she was in the village, she felt suffocated by other humans. Even with her loving family, she felt stifled. She felt everyone's feelings. If someone didn't notice their own feelings, Asira felt them even more strongly. It didn't happen every day but there were moments when a wave of something would pass over her and Asira would be overwhelmed with light or sounds and people to the point where she felt she would faint or vomit.

When the baker was mean to his son because he wanted to be a musician, Asira felt like shouting at him, "Wake up! He's so gifted! You're just disappointed he's not following you in the business." Or when Janet, the mother who had just birthed her fifth child, walked around disheveled and shuffling, Asira wanted to tell her, "Feel your melancholy and follow it deep within you until you discover the treasure that is there for you." But Asira knew they only saw her as a child of ten, not as someone wise beyond her years.

One night she got an idea. She talked to her adoptive mother and father and asked if they would help her build a small hut for herself. She would still come and help her family during the day and eat with them, but at night she would have the quiet time she so desperately craved. To her great relief, they immediately said yes, and launched into the project with great enthusiasm.

Asira knew the perfect place for her little house. Close to town, but tucked away behind some low bushes and tumbling boulders, was a little hidden corner. Two large stones leaned against each other and made ideal walls for her simple home. Her father stacked poles against the stones to create a third side, while pine branches placed on top of the poles stopped the rain from dripping inside. Smaller leafy branches interlaced among the bigger branches made the whole side water and wind-tight. The front remained open. When it was cold Asira could build a fire in front and heat up her space. The boulders absorbed the heat and then radiated it back through the night. When it was rainy, she had a tarp to pull down over the covering.

Next came the furnishings. She didn't need much. Her mother laid down some old carpets on the dirt floor. Then they brought her bed, a simple affair of slats and wooden legs. On top they placed her mattress and covers. Her father built her a small hutch with three shelves. One shelf held her clothes and the other two her plants and oils that she used in her healings. She hung baskets from the pole wall to hold the rest of her belongings. Her family blessed her new home with a simple ceremony when it was all finished. Susie gave her a lamp that Asira could use at night. It fit perfectly in a small niche in the boulders.

Her first night in her own little place Asira felt the happiest she had in a long time. She lay in her bed with her head toward the opening so she could watch the stars throughout the night. An owl swooped silently over the bushes and boulders, looking for a night snack. Just as Asira couldn't hear him, she knew he couldn't see her in her little house when the lamp was out. It made her feel safe and secure.

In the morning, Asira washed up in a little trickling stream not too far from her lean-to. She trotted off to her old home to have breakfast with her family and do her chores for the day. When she entered she felt shy at first, but everyone acted normal and didn't fuss over her after her first night alone. She relaxed and fell into the daily rhythm.

Over the coming days and nights, she was able to find a new balance within herself. The villagers had so dismissed and ignored her, it took a long time for them to notice she was living by herself. It was all so natural between Asira and her family with her living arrangement that the highly judgmental villagers couldn't find a way for their criticisms to hook into anyone. It was true what others said…out of sight was out of mind.

More animals came to her now for healing. Often times they became injured as they struggled to escape from being captured and sold to the travelers. They sensed when the villagers wanted to sell them and wouldn't come close to the village at that time. Somehow the injured ones knew where to find her. Asira spent part of her days finding the traps and dismantling them. She couldn't find all of them, though.

And so three years passed in relative harmony for Asira. But then, just as when she turned ten, she felt herself shift again. She knew it had to do with her gifts of healing. They were getting stronger and she couldn't keep them secret from the villagers. They began to ask her to heal people. Working on people was different from working on animals. The first time, she was asked to help a man with a broken leg. He was one of the travelers and Kuut, the village director, wanted him to heal and leave so he wouldn't bring bad luck to their trading. Asira wasn't sure how she could help the man, but she was afraid to say no to Kuut.

Asira approached the man hesitantly. She could see the splintered bone sticking through the man's leg. She felt the excruciating pain he was enduring in her own leg. Kuut motioned to her with a sharp gesture to start. Asira put her hands on the leg and almost fainted. Wave after wave of dizziness crashed over her. The violent spinning made her feel as if she was being lifted off the ground and spun around. She was afraid the intense vertigo would cause her to get sick on top of the man. Then she lost all sense of what was happening.

Asira awoke disoriented. She couldn't remember who she was, what day it was or even where she was. She saw a woman stirring something on the stove and a young girl sitting on a stool staring at her with wide eyes. Slowly, her sense of herself came back and she recognized Susie and then her mother. She tried to speak but could only croak. Her mother came over and handed her a hot drink. "Drink this. It'll help," she said.

Asira wrapped her hands around the hot mug and felt herself center deep within. Sipping the hot tea, she asked, "What happened?"

"You were working on a man with a broken leg," her mother replied. "Your healing powers were very strong and overcame you." With those words, Asira remembered the dizziness that had consumed her. She shuddered. She didn't want to experience that ever again.

"What happened to the man?" asked Asira.

"While your hands were on him," her mother explained, "he broke into a sweat and turned bright red all over. There was a loud crunch and his bones moved and then realigned. When he recovered from the pain he was able to get up and walk again."

"What?" exclaimed Asira. "I did that?"

"That energy that came through you certainly did," replied her mother. "But it was too much for you and after going into a trance, you passed out. Your father carried you here. That was two days ago."

Asira lay on the bed, feeling utterly weary. She hurt everywhere. Time passed and her thoughts drifted like dust specks floating in a quiet room. Someone came to the door and knocked. Asira's mother talked with them briefly, too softly for her to hear. She came over to Asira and told her the man she'd healed was at the door, wanting to thank her before he left the village. Asira shook her head. "No," she said. "Please don't let him in or make me see him." Her mother nodded and sent the man away.

Eventually Asira recovered and returned to her own home. On the surface she appeared normal as she took up her daily and nightly routines. Inside, though, she waited for the next time. And she felt more disconnected than ever from everyone else.

As the months went by and she wasn't asked to do any more healings she began to relax just a bit. Then Takaani, the wolf-dog, came into her life when he needed healing. When he was well, he didn't leave. With him and Susie by her side, life almost returned to normal.

One day the man she had healed returned to Our Place. He brought with him a young woman in fine clothes. She wasn't able to walk or even talk much because of a wasting disease. It was a miracle she'd been able to make the journey, but they had come by riverboat, faster and easier than travelling over land. They came looking for

Asira. Once again, she didn't want to do healing on any human, but Kuut demanded she do so or he'd force her family to leave the village.

When they brought Asira in front of the young woman, Asira knew immediately the problem was the young woman's heart. It wasn't an affliction from this life, though, but something that had started in another life. Hoping the horrible dizziness wouldn't reoccur, Asira placed her hands on the woman's chest.

She swayed on her feet as the dizziness immediately swept over her. Asira lost all sense of her surroundings. Behind her eyes she saw a field basking under a warm sun. There were vines being cultivated and without ever having seen them before, Asira knew they were grapes. In the distance, buildings glinted yellow and burnt orange. Asira walked barefoot in the dirt, humming happily to herself. She was excited because she was about to meet her beloved. When she was with him she didn't care that they came from different classes and that they probably didn't have a future together. It was just enough to be together. This time, though, he wasn't at their usual meeting place. She waited a while, then walked home despondently. Perhaps he'd find a way to meet her tonight at the dance in the square. Although they weren't supposed to be seen in public because neither of their families would approve, he showed up at certain times when he could. If it wasn't safe to talk, they would watch each other from across the square. It made it more fun when they did meet.

Now Asira saw herself at a dance later that night. She was looking around eagerly to find her dark and handsome lover. Suddenly on a balcony above the dance, the Duke appeared. He held his hand up for silence and everyone hushed, waiting for an important announcement.

"People of this good city," proclaimed the Duke in a booming voice. "It gives me great pleasure to announce the engagement of my son to the Countess of Lucca." Two smiling people stepped onto the balcony and waved to the cheering crowd below. Asira felt herself recoil in shock as she saw her secret love standing next to the Countess. He bent his head and kissed the woman next to him. She felt her heart crack into two despairing pieces as she fell to the cobblestones. Mercifully her vision blacked out and she couldn't see the couple or anyone at all anymore.

When Asira awoke she was back in her family's home. Her mother confirmed the young lady had been healed. Asira felt trapped by this news. She knew she was going to have more people coming to see her, and Kuut was going to make her heal them. She didn't charge anything for the healing, but Kuut did. If she stood up to him, he would punish her family.

In despair, she had her first thought of ending her life as she knew it. She never spoke the thought out loud, but her mother knew she was struggling. She told Asira to be patient and that she'd grow used to the power of her gifts of healing. But even if the horrid dizziness went away, Asira didn't like feeling the human pain. Physical pain was bad enough, but she was used to that with her animals. It was the emotional pain and mental anguish that was so torturous. So much suffering occurred in the world of humans and it was mostly caused by themselves.

Over the next six months, she did three more healings. Although her results were powerful and helped people, Asira felt herself beginning to slip away from the world. The powerful healing energy seemed to be increasing and so was the dizziness, lasting for days instead of just during the healing. More and more Asira thought of leaving the world.

The one thing that kept her still here was Takaani. Eventually she asked Susie if she'd take care of him for her. Asira told Susie she was going to take a trip and didn't want her wolf-dog to go with her. Luckily, Susie, eager to do anything for Asira, didn't question her story too much. She felt grown up taking care of Asira's beloved companion. Susie told her she'd keep a watchful eye on her little home as well while Asira was away.

"How long will you be gone?" Susie asked her.

Asira ducked her head and answered her vaguely. "Not too long," she said.

Asira knew exactly how she was going to do it. She would get close to the waterfall and just let herself drift down the river and over the edge. With the power of the water, she'd just fly away into the mist. When she heard that new travelers were on their way to see her, she knew it was time.

Her last night on Earth, Asira sat in front of her fire. She was going to send Takaani to Susie in the morning and then put her plan in action. She felt confident that if Kuut saw Takaani with her family, he'd think she was returning soon and leave her family alone. He wouldn't dare lift a hand against them with the possibility of her returning to the village at some point.

As Asira stared into the fire, she shifted into a dreamy state of inner peace. To not feel anything anymore was a relief. With a loud crack, the flames suddenly shot up. She jumped back in surprise. Within the bright flame Asira saw a vision of the Forest of Dandaka. Striding out from under the leafy canopy came a young man. He was wearing a blue cloak covered with embroidered shapes.

At the sight of him, Asira felt everything shift within her. She didn't know who he was, but she felt like she knew him. From the fire he looked straight into her eyes and in that moment she knew he was coming to help her. Her heart opened and lifted and she felt herself smile for the first time in a long time. In an instant, Asira let go of her waterfall plan. She'd wait for him to arrive. Perhaps he was coming to heal her.

CHAPTER FIVE

THE MOTHER TREE

Lan huddled in front of a small fire, his body wracked with tremors. He was wet and chilled to the bone, but burning up at the same time. His food supply had run out and there wasn't much to eat in the forest even if he were well enough to forage for food. The last several days he'd been hungry, but now he just felt empty. And weak.

Lan forced his brain to think through the heavy numbness as he roughly calculated the date. He had left the village at the end of the Maple Moon. He'd been walking for roughly two months. That meant that he was at the end of the Pecan Moon and entering the Birch Moon. This month and the next were the bitterest months of the year. Back in his village, few left the warmth of their shelters during this time. They stayed inside and took care of simple chores, repairing their tools or making new ones. It was the time of storytelling.

This most recent storm brought sleety rain that froze the tips of his ears and fingers. He'd done his best to use all the wisdom the forest had shared with him, but right now he just didn't think he could go one more step.

The weather and the lack of food had been challenge enough, but everything turned worse after his disastrous attempt to communicate with the Hawthorn tree and the thorn he'd stepped on began to fester in his foot. Eventually he wasn't able to walk and collecting wood for his fire had become almost impossible. The infection in his body seemed to affect his mind and spirit as well. A darkness had descended upon him that threatened to drag him down forever.

Feeling miserably cold, hungry and sick heightened Lan's sense of aloneness. He yearned for Boosha and the home he'd left. He hadn't felt this way in the beginning when he'd made up his mind to continue the journey at the rock pool. Back then, Lan felt excited as he learned from the forest. He'd met the Mother Tree and discovered how to connect to the root system of the forest, gain ancient information from the trunks, and receive advice from the branches.

Lan pulled the blue cloak over his head and wrapped his arms around his knees to control his trembling. As he drifted between feverish sleep and moments of awareness, he went back in time, clinging to happier memories as if it were the time of stories in his village. It kept him from being swept away by the heavy darkness. In his mind he saw the rock pool, the place he'd first eagerly embraced the new adventure and task at hand since Boosha had sent him into the forest.

With his rucksack full of food, Lan strode through the forest following the Map Compass. He hummed a song in his head as he imagined sharing his adventures with Boosha when he came home a hero. In the beginning, he loved the challenge of creating shelters at night, building fires, locating water and adding to his food supplies.

Each morning, Lan ate a little bit of his food over a cold fire. He took down his shelter and scattered the ashes just in case The Gatherers were still following him. Then he began walking, which helped warm him up. He foraged for food throughout the day as he hiked. Sometimes he found a few nuts or dried apples that other animals had missed. Some days he found mushrooms on the underside of a downed tree.

One day he discovered a boggy field of cattails. He used his digging stick to uncover dozens of the bulbous roots. That night he tossed them into his fire to cook. During the day he chewed on the knobby tubers as he walked, sucking out the starch, then spitting out the tough fibers.

Once he caught a fish with his bare hands. One of his friends in the village had shown him how to catch fish that way, but this was the first time he'd actually done it. On the bank of a small stream, staying invisible to the fish, he reached in slowly with his hand under the fish's belly. Scooping up the fish, Lan tossed him out on the river bank. Lan laughed out loud with his success. After catching a few more by hand, he roasted the fish on sticks over his fire and ate well that night.

Lan checked the Map Compass several times a day to make sure he stayed on course. After his first disastrous attempt to navigate the forest without it, he didn't know if it was wishful thinking or a deep sense of knowing that the Map Compass would keep him out of harm's way. So far he'd found the path fairly easy to hike and he hadn't seen anyone or anything threatening. He was particularly grateful there were no difficult ravines to navigate. When he had to cross a stream or creek, the Map Compass led him to a place with stones he could step across. He could almost sense where the path was without looking at the Map Compass because there was always a slight shimmer to it.

What a difference feeling warm, dry and healthy made in those early days! Months later, lying in front of his fire shivering and feverish in the dark, Lan remembered that time of wonder and delight. He spent most of his days admiring the trees around him as he walked. They were vibrantly beautiful, shining in the sunlight. His eyes never tired of feasting on the jewel-tone leaves in shades of red, orange and yellow.

As the days passed and grew shorter, the newness began to wear off. His mood shifted. Lan wished he had someone to talk to at night and share stories. What was the point of being delighted about something he'd seen or a new skill he'd mastered, if he couldn't tell anyone about it?

As his loneliness grew, his mood became grimmer. The trees that once seemed friendly and inviting now loomed over him. Sudden spurts of rain began to dominate the days and he'd grit his teeth to keep himself walking through it. The nights were getting colder and the days shorter, too. Lan had to stop earlier each day to make shelter.

In the beginning, his shelters often leaked or let the colder night air blow through. Through trial and error, Lan began developing a system that worked to keep him dry and warm. He looked for a rocky overhang or a fallen log to start with. Then he gathered branches or smaller logs to build another wall or close off the front. He stuffed grass or leaves between these logs for insulation from the wind. Finally, he looked for material, like bark from cottonwoods, to serve as shingles and ward off the rain.

Lan thought it was ridiculous to spend so much time building a shelter that he'd only use for one night and then take down the next day. He took his mounting frustration out by kicking the shelter apart each morning and stomping on the remains of his fire.

With his mood darkening, his mind began obsessing about things he didn't have answers to. He wondered how Boosha was faring and if his friends had rebuilt the village yet. If only he was home, he could show them his new skills. He also wondered about the Forest of Dandaka. Why did his village live so close to it if everyone was afraid to enter? What happened to those who ventured into the forest and never came out?

Other times he fretted about the meaning of the crystal cube called Empowerment or the Three Keys he didn't have. At his worst moments, he demanded to an unseen Boosha why he had been assigned to this task instead of someone else. When he got to that point in his downward spiral, he'd see something at the edge of his mind that he didn't want to see. Even though there was a lot of light in that corner of his mind, it scared him to look at it, so he backed away and went back to complaining about the weather. Each time he got to that point, though, it seemed bigger and scarier.

The question he circled around the most, though, was how long it would take him to get to Asira. In the beginning, he thought maybe he could complete the journey in one month (because, truthfully, that was all the time he wanted it to take). But when he checked the Map Compass each morning, he didn't seem to be making any progress at all. Slowly he realized just how vast the Forest of Dandaka was. He felt incredibly small and alone when he looked at the Map Compass, so he finally stopped wondering how long the journey would take and just focused on each day's progress.

Lately he'd begun to feel as if someone or something was watching him. Every now and then, he'd whirl around but only the trees he'd just walked past were there. He wanted to call out, "Hello, who's there?" but was afraid The Gatherers were still following him and would hear him. And that brought up more disturbing thoughts. Had they given up looking for him? He could brood on that question alone for half a day wondering what they would do if they caught him.

One morning Lan woke up late and groggy. He felt out of sorts from oversleeping, knowing he was going to have a short day of it. He sensed something had shifted in the world, but he didn't know what it was. Everything appeared the same.

Shoving his leftover dinner into his mouth, he packed and went through the motions of erasing any traces of his camp in the little hollow where he'd spent the night. Lan glumly wondered why he even bothered. It felt like forever since he'd seen or heard anyone. He almost wished The Gatherers would show up because, however bad they were, it would stop this endless loneliness.

Lan picked up his gear and started down the path because what else was he going to do? Suddenly he heard a shout in his head, "Run!" Startled, Lan bolted down the path, sprinting as fast as he could. Branches whipped him in the face and his feet bruised as he ran over sharp rocks. Part of his mind wondered what he was running from, but the panic was too big to overcome with logic. With his inner urgency cranked up to the highest level he couldn't stop and look around either.

Racing into a small clearing, he saw a magnificent tree in the center. Taller and bigger around then any tree he'd seen before, Lan ran straight to it and began climbing. The shaggy bark was hard on his palms but provided good hand and foot holds. He wasn't sure if he just wanted a place to hide or to rest. Maybe it was both.

Intent only on finding a good place to stop, Lan didn't pay much attention to the tree itself as he climbed higher. When he found a perfect bowl created by the branches separating from the trunk as they reached into the sky, he curled up into it feeling safe for the moment. All around him yellow, orange and green leaves danced slightly in the breeze. The last time he'd climbed a tree he had wanted to get high enough to see the village. This time he just wanted to stay hidden while he caught his breath and let the weird panic pass. The slight smoky smell of the tree oddly comforted him and helped slow his heart. He was just realizing that this tree was a mighty oak when his ears caught the sound of marching feet coming down the path. His heart lurched and his throat closed again. The low murmur grew louder as the group came closer.

"His tracks went this way," growled one man. "But then they disappear."

The men came right up to the tree and stood below it. Lan cautiously leaned over and looked down. The flash of red told him these men were The Gatherers and he froze, afraid they would look up and see him.

"Do we want to go back and see if he veered off or kept going on this path?" Lan looked down on the tops of their heads, but couldn't tell who was talking.

"Let's split up," said one man who towered above all the others and waved his arm. "You four go back to see if you can pick up his trail. The rest of us will continue on this path. We'll meet at last night's campsite."

After they departed, Lan lay back in his hiding spot in the tree. He'd had one of his questions answered, anyway. The Gatherers were still looking for him and they were now behind and ahead of him. How was he going to get through the forest before winter without getting caught? He slumped into the little hollow ready to give up completely.

"Fear not." Lan heard the words at the same time a leaf stroked his cheek. Startled, he looked around. Who was talking to him?

"I am," he heard. "I am the Mother Tree of the Forest of Dandaka."

When faced with a mind-boggling situation Lan always seemed to ask the stupidest questions. "Why are you the Mother Tree? Is there a Father Tree, too?"

The leaves quivered with silent laughter at his questions but the answer took him by surprise. "I can tell you why I'm the Mother Tree, but asking about a Father Tree is the wrong question. Would you like to know more about me?"

Lan felt "yes" swell up from his entire being and burst out of his mouth. At first he just thought he was desperate to talk to someone, but then as he learned more about the Mother Tree he realized that many of his daily questions were being answered as well.

"I am the Mother Tree because I am the oldest tree in the Forest of Dandaka. My rings carry all history, such as the bad times when humans almost cut us down to nothing, and the times of the Great Shift with the raging fires, winds and earth shaking. My rings also know the weather patterns and the best time to send out new leaves and when to let them go. It is a delicate dance every year."

For once Lan didn't have any questions to hide behind. Although he could hear the words being spoken by the Mother Tree, he was also being shown what she was talking about.

"When our home stopped shaking and blowing, something had changed inside of us. We had learned how to protect ourselves from humans or anyone who wished to harm us. Now only those who honor and protect us can pass through."

Lan flashed back to the dead Gatherers. He wondered if this is what the Mother Tree meant about protecting themselves, but then he thought about the ones who had just passed and were still looking for him. "Don't worry, we will take care of them as well," he heard her say softly.

As the day continued, the Mother Tree taught Lan about herself and the Forest. She showed him how the branches and leaves communed with the sun, wind and clouds while they magically made food. The trunks operated like a super road where food travelled down to the roots, and water and nutrients travelled up from the dirt. He learned how the trees connected to other trees through their roots and a white stringy fungi and sent food and water to other trees to help them. He saw how a tree that had been cut down could keep living from the help of its neighbors, even when it didn't have leaves to create food for itself.

The Mother Tree's job was to work with all the new saplings. She taught them forest history and how to receive nurturing from the sun and the stars, their loamy home and from the other trees.

Lan fell asleep in the arms of the Mother Tree, feeling as if he continued the conversation in his dreams. He never felt thirsty or hungry as he realized that his conversation with her had nourished him just as she fed the saplings.

In the morning, the Mother Tree said, "I have one more thing to share with you. Come within me."

Lan felt himself sink into her trunk. He saw the inside of her filled with crystalline rings that gave off the shimmery light he saw when he was walking through the forest. Then she took him further into her roots and he found himself flying through the underground grid system. He had no idea where they were going until they ended up right in the middle of his village under the large tree that everyone gathered under. He was not far from his home with Boosha.

Suddenly he saw Boosha above him walk into their hut. He tried to call out to her but got a mouthful of dirt. Even so, she stopped, turned and looked around sharply. Then a smile formed on her face and she waved to the tree. Something deep within Lan released as he realized how worried he'd been about her. He knew that his journey could take as long as it needed. Then just as fast as he'd travelled through the roots to the village he was back again in the tree bowl.

"It's time to go. I have a special treat waiting for you with the birches so be sure to spend the night with them." Once again Lan saw a picture with the Mother Tree's words. A beautiful grove of white birches, complete with a pile of dead branches in the middle, appeared in his mind.

Climbing down, Lan put his arms around the massive trunk of the Mother Tree although he could only reach part way. "Thank you," he said. The words didn't seem adequate for all her help and wisdom. "I promise to protect and honor the trees."

"On you go then," she said and Lan felt himself pushed down the trail. His mood was light once again as he got back into his walking rhythm. He saw no signs of The Gatherers as he strode on the trail and his fear that they would find him disappeared.

A day later he came upon the birch grove. In the center was a pile of branches exactly how he'd been shown by the Mother Tree. After he started a fire, he cooked some mushrooms and made tea with the birch twigs. He didn't know why he was supposed to be there, but maybe the birches would show him things like the Mother Tree had. Lying back on some crunchy dried leaves that smelled refreshingly minty, Lan looked up the trunks and into the branches. The trees rose tall and straight in the air with black markings that made their white bark stand out in stark contrast. Their canopy of tear-drop leaves with serrated edges were mostly yellow now, though a few were still green.

As night descended, Lan sat dreamily in front of the fire. His eyes began to droop. Suddenly he felt a weird sensation in his legs. Looking down he saw roots growing from his legs and feet, burying themselves deep into the ground. Before he could even comprehend what was happening his arms rose over his head, becoming branches with leaves sprouting from them. His body had become a pure white trunk. He shook his head, wondering if it was the result of the mushrooms he'd eaten or a dream, but nothing changed. He had turned into a tree!

Then his dream got stranger. While he had become rooted to the spot, the birch trees were walking around! Lan stood up and discovered he could pull his roots out of the ground by lifting first one knee, then the other into the air. He began tree-walking like the other trees. It was cumbersome walking on roots instead of feet, but he loved being so tall and taking long steps. While he was learning to manage his root feet, the trees began dancing. Moving in graceful sweeps and bows, they circled around the grove.

Lan was filled with an intense desire to dance as well, but when he tried to move like the other trees, he immediately tripped over his roots. Shame and embarrassment swept through him with his clumsiness, a familiar feeling. One of the trees came up to him and shook her leaves over his roots. Oddly it felt like his root-feet were being washed. Unexpectedly, old memories surfaced from his childhood.

He saw the hurt from traumatic events stored in his roots. There was the time an older boy had mocked him for having no parents and living with old Boosha. Another time a group of kids picked up stones and threw them at a dog that had wandered through the village. Lan tried to stop them and they threw the stones at him instead. And then he saw himself right after his parents were taken away. He was a baby and not even talking yet. Most villagers thought he hadn't realized his parents were gone, but he had. His roots stored all those feeling-memories. As more birch trees cleansed his roots the tortured feelings began to wash away.

With the root clearing, Lan began to dance like the other trees. He felt himself connect to his elemental self. Through his roots, he took in water, minerals and an energy that he didn't have a name for, but that filled his body with a special power. He felt vitally alive and strong.

Now he wanted to wave his arm-branches as he danced, but they felt heavy and burdened. A tree near him bent down and whispered, "Gavilan." He didn't know what that meant, other than the word on his Map Compass. Tree after tree came up to him and whispered the same word. Each time, Lan felt stronger and more sure of himself, odd because he had no idea what was going on.

The last tree lifted Lan's arm-branches just as the hawk from the ravine flew overhead. He felt awash in an incredible nectar of love. Moonlight flowed into his leaves, then branches. He trembled with joy as his leafy branch-arms waved in sweeping gestures.

His root-legs danced and his arm-branches waved, but his trunk-body felt incredibly stiff. His bark-skin was too tight. Though his trunk did not show one black blemish, he felt marred and imperfect because of the way the villagers had seen him. Lan remembered times when he'd desperately tried to show other villagers his strong sense of self from his roots and the incredible love in his branches, but they had turned away in disgust.

In the grove, trees came up around him and began to hit him on his body-trunk. Each time they hit him a black mark formed. The more whacks he got, the more he felt his root energy rise up and his leafy-branch energy flow down. The two energies mingled in his trunk, making the most exquisite sap within him, pouring out of the black wounds in huge waves of relief and happiness. Looking at the black marks on the other trees, Lan realized everyone had wounds they were ashamed of, not just himself.

The other trees encouraged him to dance as they circled around him in what he could only call tree hugging. His trunk energy combined with the others and together they created a beautiful tapestry of light. As the dance increased in wildness, he felt a homecoming that he had never felt before. How weird he had to become a tree to feel like a young man! He danced exuberantly, swept up in the energy of earth, trees, and starry heavens.

Lan woke to the warmth of the sunlight on his face. By the position of the sun, he knew it was late morning. He didn't want to get up yet, but rather stay in his dream from the night before. He stretched his branches toward the sun, then realized they were simply human arms again. He looked down and saw that he had legs. Lan's gaze swept around the birch grove. Once again, they were still and completely rooted to the earth, only now there wasn't one single leaf on them. On the ground swirls of leaves still danced as they lifted in the wind.

Was it a dream or was it real, he wondered? Something made him lift up his shirt and he saw welts all over his stomach and chest. Although they were lighter in color, they were the same shapes as the dark markings on the birch trunks. They looked like a type of bruise, but it hadn't hurt when the trees had hit him and the bruises didn't hurt now. Still, he had proof that the wild night of tree dancing had actually happened.

Expecting to feel sore, Lan rose and packed up his gear, then cleared up his campsite. He didn't feel sore at all and in fact had never felt so good in his life. Looking down at his skin he saw that it shimmered a little, like the trees.

"Thank you," Lan said before leaving the grove. He sent a silent "thank you" into the roots in the ground back to the Mother Tree. He knew he had truly become part of the tree tribe. In the coming days, most of the markings from his body disappeared, but a few stayed and slowly turned a dark brown. The sight of them would always remind him of the night he became a tree in a wild dance.

Returning to the bleaker reality from his memories of happier times, Lan reached out and put one of the last branches on the fire. What a different blaze this one was compared to the birch bonfire. Now the dark overcast night pressed down on the meager fire, threatening to put it out completely. The leafless trees had gone to sleep and weren't communicating with him. Lan knew he needed to gather more logs so they could dry out before he put them on the fire, but he was too weak to move. Trying not to worry about what he was going to do in the coming days and to avoid how awful he felt, Lan retreated into his memories again.

During the days after the birch dance, Lan felt like he had entered a school and the trees were his teachers. When one of them wanted to teach him something, it would draw his attention in some way. One time a great branch fell right in his path. Another time the light would shine on just one tree in the midst of others. One tree drew his attention through the raucous cries of dozens of jays sitting in the branches.

Gradually he realized that these signs weren't random but tied in with his thoughts and questions. Once he understood that, his communication with the trees increased tenfold. He just had to put his hand on the tree that had signaled him and he would travel into the roots, back up to the branches and then shift into the trunk to understand what they were showing him.

In this way, he met Alder, who helped to rebuild the forest after the Great Shift. Maple showed him how it found underground water, while White Spruce created cover for the small animals in wintertime. Crabapple shared with him the image of its flowers that caught starlight in each petal, and Aspen showed how its grove was one living organism. Hickory was all about strength and knew its wood was prized for making many tools that lasted a long time. Mountain Ash put a lot of energy into its brilliant berries to hide its sensitivity. If something was off throughout the forest, Mountain Ash knew immediately. Chokecherry had flowers similar to Crabapple and delighted in feeding the birds. Cypress loved the edges of streams and had to stand taller than the other trees to connect the energies between earth and heaven. It knew what kind of weather was coming. Each tree had a sense of itself and of its place in the forest, making it strong and protected. As Lan drank in the tree wisdom, he was also nurtured through their energy. He didn't need as much food when he talked with the trees.

Gradually all the trees lost their leaves while their shimmery energy went to sleep in their roots. Lan found he couldn't tap into them for his own daily energy boost. The weather continued to worsen and his feet grew heavier with every step. He made less progress every day.

One day he came to a hawthorn tree. It still had all its leaves and even bright berries. It was a sore sight for Lan's eyes against the backdrop of sleeping, grey trees. It didn't shimmer with light like the other trees but had a certain hard glitter to it. Although something inside of him shivered, Lan approached the tree hoping to communicate with it and receive some energy. The tree drew him in but did not seem as welcoming as the others. This was the first hawthorn Lan had met, so he thought maybe it was just different from all the rest of the trees. As always, he planned to ask permission before proceeding to honor it.

Tentatively he placed his hand on the trunk. He began to merge with the trunk of the tree as he asked it permission to communicate. For a brief moment, he saw a room with two individuals sitting at a table. They looked up, startled, then there was a blast of energy and he was flung violently backward. His foot came down on a wickedly long thorn that pierced his shoe straight through his foot. From above, the tree rained down more thorns. Throwing an arm over his face, Lan rolled over and tried to stand up, but the pain in his foot was agonizing. Crying out, he dropped to all fours and crawled away as quickly as he could to get out of range of the flying thorn missiles. Finally, he stopped and, biting his lip to stop from crying out, pulled the thorn out. It was covered with his blood and little pieces of tissue. He felt faint at the sight of it but the throbbing in his foot kept him all too present.

Lan's mind shattered. What had just happened? Why had the tree responded so violently against him? He looked at the Map Compass, only to see it had gone blank again. His heart sank. Now he had more problems than before. Moving further away from the tree, Lan decided to stop for the night. He only had enough energy to build a fire and collect some wood before collapsing in front of it. In the morning, he'd figure it all out somehow.

But in the morning, the Map Compass still didn't work and he felt worse than before. Lan's one night turned into two and then five. On this bitterly cold night he put the last of his wood on the fire and fell into a fitful sleep. Unaware any more of where he was or what he needed to do next, he sank into the darkness that pulled him down and wouldn't let him go.

CHAPTER SIX

SAFE HAVEN

In a high-ceilinged room in front of a massive burning fire, Draegan Osuro read under a floating glass bulb. He seemed mildly entertained with what he was reading. Overlord of the World Regime, His Excellency's long, white hair was brushed back from his face, but hung scruffily over his collar. Despite the image his mottled, puffy face and thickened waist conveyed, he held the power of a coiled snake ready to strike with tremendous speed and accuracy. No one wanted to disappoint this man and face the consequences. Even the room seemed to pull back from him as the dark wood paneling absorbed all available light and sound. The weight of the stillness bore down on everything.

Tarek, the Chief Informer, slid through the door, checking to see if he would be interrupting His Excellency. Before Tarek could clear his throat or talk, Draegan spoke without looking up.

"Yes, what is it?"

"The tripwire in the Forest of Dandaka has been detonated," Tarek replied.

Although he barely moved, something snapped into deadly focus within Draegan. His eyes locked intently onto Tarek, who shifted back and forth on his feet.

"Is it The Awakener?" Draegan asked neutrally.

"I can't quite tell," Tarek answered uneasily. "It doesn't read as a Crystalline or as The Awakener."

Draegan exploded out of his seat, his hands thundering down on the desk. "Then why are you bothering me with this information?"

Tarek nervously took one step back. "Because the tree was set to detonate only if The Awakener or a Crystalline found it. But it was set so long ago…do we even know if it is still working right?"

"Well, can you tell if it was detonated by a person or an animal or even a storm?" Draegan asked.

"I'm pretty sure it was a person. I'm almost positive about that." Tarek backtracked with his words as he had with his body. He wasn't sure which was worse with Draegan…being overly confident and then wrong, or just uncertain.

"Could you look at the Glyph and see what you think?" Tarek's voice broke at the end. He didn't want to seem like a coward, but standing up to Draegan was always a risk.

For now, Draegan's mood seemed calmly controlled as he followed Tarek out of the office. Together they crossed a common area and entered a different doorway, into a bare room with curved, paneled walls. From a distance what appeared to be framed art hung from each panel. As Tarek and Draegan got closer to the hangings they became sculptures of trees, rocks, buildings and landscapes.

Although beautiful, they exuded a strange energy, glittering with a dark light that drew the viewer in. These were Glyphs, traps set in the world for a specific purpose. Draegan and Tarek approached the first one at the far left. It contained a tree that looked damaged.

Only two people in the world knew that if a Crystalline touched that particular tree in the forest, it would fall into geometric shapes. If The Awakener touched the tree, it would stay standing but become a hollow shell. Draegan and Tarek stood in front of the image of the tree, studying it.

Draegan reached into his pocket, took out a small silver box, opened it and took out a pinch of dark brown powder, sniffing it up his nose. He waited for his brain to charge, then closed his eyes and connected to the Dark Grid, asking to mentally travel to the tree. He scanned the area but didn't see anyone. The tree looked as if it had been struck by lightning from within. Draegan noticed something at the foot of the tree and picked it up, studying it. He came back to the Glyph room with Tarek and said, "Someone laid another tripwire over the first one. It warned them and covered up ours. Reset each of the tripwires in the Glyphs, and check for any outside energies overlaying them. Let me know if you find any more."

Tarek nodded his head and started to move to the next frame, but Draegan wasn't finished. "Where is the closest village to this tree?" he asked.

"I believe it's the village called Our Place," Tarek responded. "The director is Kuut.

"Fine," said Draegan. "Send The Gatherers there and search for any Crystallines or those who are harboring Crystallines. Make an example of someone."

Tarek nodded again, knowing he was about to rain down terror on an unsuspecting town. He wouldn't want to be in their shoes.

Lan swirled down into darkness. He had no sense of time or place. All around him spun despair and hopelessness. Occasionally he glimpsed and heard strangers talking about things he didn't understand. Once he saw two men in a round room looking at a tree sculpture. He heard the words "The Awakener" as he floated passed them. He had no idea who they were talking about but he instinctively tried to hide himself, terrified they would see him. Then he saw a village being burned down and two people running away from it. He felt scared for those people. Other times in the consuming darkness, horrible-looking creatures laughed and pointed at his helplessness. They seemed to be eating something that was coming from him. His heart pounded in his ears as he tried to push them away.

Occasionally he fought against the darkness and would find himself in a room filled with light. He felt his limbs bathed in cool water by someone he couldn't see, which relieved his fevered and achy body. At those times, he tried to completely escape the darkness, but he couldn't quite manage it. As soon as Lan tired, it would pull him under again.

One day Lan opened his eyes. He was lying in front of a fire in a room that reminded him of home. He was filled with such emptiness that he had no curiosity about where he was or how he got there. The door flung open and a man entered with his arms full of firewood. He glanced at Lan and his face lit up with a smile. "Welcome back!" he said as he strode toward the fireplace and unceremoniously dumped the wood on the floor. "How are you feeling?"

Lan opened his mouth to speak but found his voice didn't work. Only a garbled squawk came out. Startled, he realized it had been quite a while since he'd spoken with another person. With that thought, the memories of the past several months came roaring back into his awareness. He flashed back on Boosha asking him to take the Three Keys and the Crystal Cube through the forest. He remembered trying to find his own way and meeting obstacle after obstacle. He relived the joy of travelling through the forest as he followed the path, and communed with the trees. He saw himself so sick he couldn't move after the hawthorn tree blasted him and he'd stepped on the thorn. Then his memories stopped.

Lan pulled his blanket up and looked at his foot. A scar crossed the top and bottom but when he wiggled his foot, it didn't hurt at all. The rest of his body was another story. He felt like the morning after the windy night in the rocky ravine again.

The man offered him water. After taking several sips Lan managed to croak out, "Where am I?"

"You're still in the Forest of Dandaka," replied the man. "My name is Sawyer and I brought you here after finding you passed out.

You were unconscious for quite a while.

Finding it tiring to talk, Lan tried to nod his head but it seemed the smallest movement wore him out. In the coming days, he managed to stay awake longer as Sawyer fed him simple broths and teas. He also bathed Lan with a special water sprinkled with salt. Lan felt embarrassed to be bathed by a man he didn't know, but the relief to his body was so immediate Lan never asked him to stop.

As Lan's strength slowly returned, Sawyer sometimes wrapped him in blankets then carried him outside to sit in the sun. The cottage, almost completely hidden on the edge of a meadow, barely even showed smoke from the chimney. Lan didn't recognize this part of the forest. The trees didn't speak to him. After weeks of communing only with the forest, it felt strange to be so disconnected.

Although it was still winter and the sun wasn't that strong, Lan felt strengthened by it. After spending so much time under the forest canopy, then the overcast and rainy weather, Lan had almost forgotten there was a sun.

In the beginning, Lan was too weak to do anything but watch Sawyer while he chopped wood or made cordage from different plant fibers. Normally, Lan would have had a hundred questions for him but the emptiness within him extended to his mind as well. He watched Sawyer work without any curiosity. It felt strange to be with another human again. He'd forgotten the right responses.

Lan felt disconnected not only from life around him, but also himself. A black shadow overlay his mind, robbing his perceptions of color. Normal activities seemed pointless. He didn't think about the past and what led him here, or the future and what he was supposed to do next. The timeframe of his life shrank to just the daily activities of waking, eating, bathing and going back to sleep.

One day, Sawyer began teaching Lan how to make cordage. Working with dogbane, he showed Lan how to hand crush the stem and divide it, peeling off the fiber from the bark and inner pulpy material, and then twisting and weaving it into cords. Lan felt a flicker of excitement in his mind as he learned a new skill, but then quickly grew frustrated with his weakness. He only lasted several minutes with his first attempt before his arms grew too heavy to continue. If he could have found a way to say no to Sawyer he would have, but Sawyer just seemed to overlook how helpless he was at the task.

In spite of his dark mood, Lan began to make some progress. His stamina and speed for making cordage picked up. His twisting and weaving efforts began to produce beautiful strong cord. When Lan had a good supply made, Sawyer shifted to a new project. He began teaching Lan different things to make with the cordage, including snares to catch rabbits. These went into their stews. Lan didn't care for meat much and really didn't like butchering the rabbits, but his body craved the protein-rich stews as it continued healing.

Next, they began making arrowheads. After collecting a pile of rocks, Sawyer showed Lan how to strike one against another to get razor sharp edges. After that, they shaped the fragments into the right size with pointy tips and notches at the base. Eventually they made shafts that were straight and strong. Lan never questioned

Sawyer why he was doing these tasks. He figured it was just what Sawyer did every day and he was getting extra help from Lan.

After he'd made a dozen arrows and a quiver to hold them, Sawyer showed Lan how to make a bow, stringing it with more cordage. Shooting the arrow for the first time, Lan felt excited, a welcome relief from the emptiness he normally felt. But his weakness showed up again and the arrow landed just a few feet in front of him. He threw the bow down with disgust and stalked away. Sawyer didn't respond except to bring him back to target practice the next day.

Now he had a new task to help him rebuild his strength as he worked each day with his bow and arrows. They mostly worked in silence with Sawyer showing Lan through his actions how to do something new. Lan never understood how Sawyer knew exactly when to break the silence and share a gentle tip with Lan to get better accuracy or distance.

His days were marked by the slow progress of his recovery. Sometimes he seemed to make big leaps and then the following day regress. Gradually, Lan noticed a pattern related to his sleep. When Lan slept without remembering his dreams he was able to make more progress with his tasks. Other nights he returned again and again to the black swirling place. The figures that appeared out of the darkness were always terrifying as they taunted him with their wide gaping mouths and hands that reached out to grab him. When he reacted in fear they expanded in size. He dreaded these nightmares.

Lan's fear of falling asleep at night had two effects. First, Lan began to truly despise himself. He'd always doubted himself because he seemed so different from the other villagers, but now that doubt intensified and he began to believe he was some kind of freak. He hated it. This feeling wrapped around the dark shadow in his mind and he couldn't tell which one came first. When he woke after a bad night of terror, his first thought was always, "I hate myself."

The second effect was that Lan began to reach out in conversation to Sawyer at night in an effort to delay going to bed. After dinner was cooked and eaten and the kitchen cleaned up, they sat in front of the fire drinking tea. In the beginning, Lan would droop with tiredness and didn't last very long. But as his strength returned he was able to stay awake longer.

One night he asked, "How long was I sick?"

"Almost a month."

Sawyer's short answer forced Lan to dig for more information. "Well, how did you find me?"

"There was a disturbance in the Golden Grid and I went to find out what it was," Sawyer replied.

This startled Lan so much, he forgot what he was going to ask next. Someone else knew about the Golden Grid that he'd seen when he was flying in Hawk's body! Although Lan felt more connected to the Forest after his Hawk time, he'd never seen the Golden Grid again, not even when he was Tree Talking. Lan wanted more information but he didn't even know what to ask. It took him another day of thinking to start asking Sawyer new questions.

"Do you see the Golden Grid all the time?" Lan asked him the next night as they sat in front of the fire, drinking birch tea.

"Yes and no," Sawyer answered. "After seeing it several times, I was able to sense it with my body so I mostly use that. To see it, I have to shift my focus from a sensing mode into a seeing mode."

Lan fell silent, trying to understand what Sawyer had just said. Had Lan sensed the Golden Grid after the Hawk journey? That led him to his next question. "How do you know when you are sensing it?"

As always, Sawyer's answer was even with no hint of impatience. "I'm aware of the aliveness of everything. The trees, birds, insects, rocks, soil, plants, water. It's a sense of connection with the All That Is and a connection to each individual part. We commune through this connection."

Lan took another day to think about this answer. He remembered how he felt walking through the forest and his wonderful Tree Talks. Was he connected to the Golden Grid then? If he had been, he certainly didn't feel that connection anywhere inside of him now. Lan didn't understand it all, but just thinking about the Golden Grid helped to lift the shadowy veil off his mind. He could almost glimpse his old self.

Lan began to eagerly look forward to each evening when he and Sawyer continued talking. No question seemed too stupid for Sawyer. Sometimes Sawyer's answers didn't seem to answer his initial question but addressed something deeper that Lan wasn't aware he'd wanted to ask.

"Why did you shift from seeing to sensing?" Lan asked.

Sawyer answered, "It saves energy." Sawyer seemed to save

energy with everything, including his answers.

Lan puzzled about Sawyer. He wasn't like anyone Lan had ever met. Sawyer was quiet but not because he didn't talk much. He obviously preferred showing over telling, but there was something else about his quietness that was new to Lan. He would have asked Sawyer about it, but he didn't know how to put it into words. Lan was only able to put his finger on the difference when he compared Sawyer to the other villagers he knew. They were loud with their energy, especially their emotions. They threw their feelings around like an invisible wave, pushing or smothering or holding others down. Like his home, Sawyer blended perfectly with the trees, rocks or any background. When he approached a rabbit caught in a snare, Sawyer first calmed the rabbit and then did something with his hands and eyes that Lan could only call a blessing before killing it. In Sawyer's hands, death wasn't violent but a natural part of life.

Because Sawyer was so quiet, Lan felt himself coming out of the dark state of mind and the self-loathing that sucked him down every night. He began reaching out for something that he needed, but that had no name. It was like drinking water without realizing he'd been thirsty.

One day Lan realized that Sawyer had never called him by his name. In fact, Sawyer hadn't even asked him his name. That night, Lan finished cleaning up after the nightly meal with an eagerness he hadn't shown before. As soon as they sat down in front of the fire, he asked Sawyer, "How come you've never asked me my name?"

"I already know your name," Sawyer replied calmly.

"What? What do you think my name is?" Lan asked as a rush of his emotions spilled into the room.

Sawyer didn't react to the edgy, impatient energy. He smiled slightly and, looking directly at Lan said, "You're Gavilan."

Lan felt his mouth fall open when he heard that word come out of Sawyer's mouth. He sat stunned, amazed that Sawyer would even speak the name, but then was even more shocked when he suddenly connected the dots. The "Gavilan" on the Map Compass, the "Gavilan" in the branches of his birch tree—somehow, they were him. Then he realized that his name Lan was part of Gavilan. His brain couldn't take in any more surprises and shut down. Mumbling "Good night," he crawled into his bed and pulled the covers over his head. That night he didn't have the nightmare of the creatures in the dark, whirling space. He didn't dream at all.

In the morning, Lan stretched and noticed how much better he felt. Then the strange conversation from the night before rushed back into his mind. He picked up his rucksack from the floor and searched for the Map Compass. He hadn't looked at it since it had stopped working after the violent blast of the hawthorn tree. He wondered if it was working now and if he'd see his name on it. But the Map Compass remained blank. New questions rushed into his mind. Was it broken forever? How would he finish Boosha's task or find his way back to her without it? He put it away and went outside, hoping. he'd figure it out later.

After a day of making birch boxes and pine pitch glue, Lan determined to stay up as long as Sawyer did and get the answers to all the questions that were spilling out of his head.

"How do you know my name? And I mean, how did you know my name is Gavilan when even I didn't know my name is Gavilan, and how do you know who I am?"

Sawyer took his time before answering, stirring up the logs and pouring more tea. He settled more deeply into his chair.

"I came to your village just after your parents were taken away by The Gatherers," Sawyer started quietly.

With that information, Lan jumped slightly in his chair and started to speak, but Sawyer held up his hand.

"Let me tell you my story first, then you can ask me whatever else you want to know."

Lan hadn't realized how desperate he was for more information about his parents until Sawyer stopped him from asking. He settled into his chair and tried to make himself as quiet as Sawyer.

"When I arrived at your village, everyone was still in a state of shock. Some of the homes had been burnt to the ground and people were injured. I came to the village looking for Boosha because we knew each other before Zero Point."

Lan opened his mouth at the words "Zero Point" but then shut it when Sawyer held up his hand again. He kept quiet but squirmed in his seat.

"Boosha and I didn't have much time for catching up," Sawyer continued. "She needed someone to stay with you so she could heal the villagers. In the beginning, then, I took care of you."

Lan searched his mind for some memory of this but nothing

came up. Sawyer continued, "You were an easy baby to take care of. You were quiet, and ate and slept well. The chaos of the village didn't seem to affect you much."

As if anticipating Lan's next question, Sawyer said, "I was there two winters. During the winter months, Boosha and I talked about your future. We knew there would come a time when you had to make this journey, so I moved here to be ready for you."

Lan's mind raced over the revelation that all of this had been planned for him. Why was the journey so important? Every new piece of information just seemed to lead him to more questions. Just like on that day Boosha sent him into the forest, Lan's whole sense of his life kept shattering around him.

"If you're wondering why The Gatherers didn't take you as well as your parents," Sawyer continued, "it's because The Gatherers didn't realize you'd been born yet. Their time line was off and they thought your parents were still childless. When they came for your parents, Boosha was taking care of you while they went looking for certain plants in the forest. Your parents were scientists, experimenting with different plants to heal certain illnesses. When The Gatherers came and threatened to burn down every house in the village and hurt or even kill people if they didn't tell them where your parents were, Boosha was the one who sent them to the forest."

At this news, Lan felt his throat contract. His beloved Boosha had actually betrayed his parents. His eyes welled up with tears. Then he felt a fiery rage rise within him and his tears became diamond hard. "Fortcate them all!" he thought. For his entire life, the absence of his parents had always lurked in the background. He felt loved by Boosha, but there existed this uncomfortable energy between him and others in the village that he never understood. People went out of their way to smile at him and offer treats, but their eyes would shift away when he responded with his own smile.

Sawyer nodded sympathetically at Lan as if he could hear his thoughts. "To be honest, Boosha never thought they'd actually find your parents. We're not sure how they did, but if they hadn't, they would have come back to the village and done more damage. Everyone, except Boosha, was secretly hoping The Gatherers would find your parents. This might have been why your parents let themselves be captured, to save the village. More importantly, they wanted to lead them away from you.

"Don't be mad at Boosha or the villagers," Sawyer cautioned him. "Boosha was doing what your parents had told her to do, even though she didn't want to. And the villagers were just being human. If humans aren't awakened, they respond to everything from a survival level. At that level, it's you versus them. Every tyrant knows that by creating fear and dividing people against each other, he can control everyone much easier. The Gatherers are meant to spread fear and divide people as much as they are to take some people away."

At some point, Lan noticed that he wasn't paying as much attention to Sawyer's words as he was to the pictures in his mind. Not just pictures, but also feelings. When Sawyer was talking about The Gatherers coming to the village, Lan saw them thundering in and overrunning everyone with their shouts and demands. He felt the fear and panic rush through the villagers. When Sawyer talked about Boosha showing them where his parents had gone, he saw her stand in front of the leader and point to the forest. At the same time, he felt Boosha's heavy heart in the action. The villagers, though, simply felt relief that it was someone else The Gatherers went after and glad that Boosha had been the one to show them. They felt shame about being such cowards and not standing up for their fellow kin. In the following days and years, the sight of Lan reminded them of how eager they had been to sacrifice his parents and they felt guilty when they looked at him.

Sawyer continued his story. He seemed to know what Lan was understanding and brought in new information to answer Lan's questions before his mind even formulated them. "Boosha and I decided to change your name so that the villagers weren't reminded of that day every time they looked at you or heard your name. We stopped calling you Gavilan and only referred to you as Lan."

Now that Lan knew his full name was Gavilan, it seemed so obvious the two names were connected he had a hard time believing that Boosha and Sawyer thought changing his name to Lan would work. The picture feelings in his mind showed him Sawyer holding him as a baby, then making a motion with his hand, much like the gesture he used with the rabbits before killing them. Except he didn't kill Lan with the motion, just erased all memory of that horrible day and the knowledge that his real name was Gavilan. Most of the villagers forgot about his connection to that terrible day, but it didn't stop them from feeling guilty whenever they looked at him. They just didn't know why.

Lan was so overcome with sadness for that young baby and then himself as a boy he felt like a sack of rocks sitting in the chair. Through the picture-feelings he saw himself bright and curious, approaching everyone with the same love that his parents had given him. Their response was to pull away and brush him off. He saw the young boy in pain and confusion when they didn't receive his love. His young brain reasoned they rejected him because he didn't have parents and that there was something shameful about that.

As Lan realized that all this time he'd thought there was something wrong with him because of some of the villagers' responses, the sadness was replaced with a great anger. The fiery rage made him spring out of his chair. Not able to contain himself any longer, he rushed outside and ran across the starlit meadow. At the edge of the forest, just as he had that first day he escaped from The Gatherers, he tripped on the root of a tree. He shouted out with the shock of falling and then deep sobs broke from his chest and belly. Wrapping his arms around the tree, he felt a deep yearning to be hugged by his own parents. He wept with the heartbreak of the loss of those two people he'd never known or remembered. After a long time of sobbing and striking the trunk with his fists, he finally sat down at the base of the tree feeling empty and bereft. Being an orphan in the world was a weight on him that made everything seem impossible. He whispered, "I can't do this, don't ask me."

A branch, showing signs of the coming spring with its unopened leaf buds, stroked his face. It sparked a new set of picture-feelings. He saw his parents preparing for a day when they might have to protect him by leaving. His mother's love and nurturing were transferred to Boosha when his mother gave her a special plant for her garden. Boosha had used that plant in their teas. Lan's love of daydreaming came from his mother, who had also adored watching the butterflies in the forest. His father's kindness and teachings were passed to Sam, the blacksmith, and to John, the woodworker, who mentored Lan as he grew up.

Then Lan saw a most startling picture-feeling. Sawyer had known his parents before they'd moved to the village! They bestowed their parenting gifts on him as well. Boosha and Sawyer were the only two, though, who fully understood the exchange and what it meant. Lan suddenly inhaled and felt the hole in his heart that had always been there fill with a golden substance. He not only had been loved by his parents, but he'd always been connected to them across space and time. This revelation was so amazing, Lan stayed by the tree long into the night, afraid to move in case the connection disappeared. The cold air finally drove him back to the cottage. He crept in quietly, not wanting to wake Sawyer.

That night he fell into the dark spiral again, but this time when the ugly, grasping entities reached out to him, laughing and pointing fingers, Lan only felt the love he'd been surrounded with all his life. It poured out of his heart and radiated in a golden light all around him. The dark creatures pulled away and shrieked as though the light burned them.

In his sleep, Lan smiled. He knew they just needed to find their own source of love.

CHAPTER SEVEN

UNDER THE DOUBLE FULL MOON

"You're ready," Sawyer said to Lan.

Lan looked up from the fire. He was making another batch of maple syrup in one of their birch containers. They had started a few days earlier tapping the trees for sap. Spring was definitely on its way. Nights were still cold but days were warming up. It was the perfect combination for the sap to start running from the roots to the branches in the maples and birches. Sawyer's process was simple. Make a V-shaped cut in the trunks with his knife and place a concave piece of bark in the notch at a downward angle. Underneath the bark spigot he placed a birch bucket. In the beginning, it took a couple of days to fill a bucket but as the days got warmer, they began to fill more quickly. Sawyer encouraged Lan to drink the sap as a spring tonic. It gave him a boost in energy. The rest of the sap they turned into syrup.

Sawyer spoke to Lan just as he was navigating a hot rock from the fire with a forked stick to place in the birch bucket. The hot rocks cooked the sap into a thicker syrup. Sawyer would also leave the sap out at night. The water would rise to the top and freeze, to be removed in the day. Between rock cooking in the day and freezing at night, the syrup developed a smooth texture and intense flavor. They stored the finished product in Sawyer's root cellar with tight lids to keep out insects.

Lan stopped his process of picking up a hot rock with two sticks. He wasn't sure what startled him more...that Sawyer said something unrelated to the task at hand, or the words themselves. Regardless, he needed his full attention to pick up a hot rock with two sticks. Now he concentrated on Sawyer's words. What was he ready for? Was it time for him to leave? Or did Sawyer have something else he wanted to share with him?

Since the night Lan had conquered the night terrors, his relationship with Sawyer had changed. Lan no longer felt like an outsider or a patient who was being nursed back to wellness. Sawyer wasn't a random stranger who had happened to save him in the woods, but family. Lan began to trust Sawyer with his whole heart and mind. The journey felt more planned and less random. Whatever Sawyer had to teach him served a bigger purpose and Lan didn't even have to know what it was. It was enough that Sawyer knew. Lan soaked up Sawyer's wisdom with every part of his being.

After Sawyer's announcement, they went back to making maple syrup in silence, but the next day Sawyer started showing Lan how to move his energy. Sawyer talked about the three energy seats in the body and how they were the loudest of all of the energies. Sawyer explained that each one could be used to great effect when Lan needed it, but if not controlled, they warned everyone that he was approaching or made him vulnerable to being controlled and manipulated. To life connected to the Golden Grid, loud energy meant someone wasn't listening or was out of harmony. Those not connected weren't able to receive help or support and were sometimes attacked for lack of understanding.

Lan took all this in without too many questions. Sawyer wasn't just giving him information but also demonstrating. In the meadow in front of the house, Sawyer showed him the location of the three energy seats of the body. The first one sat in his low belly. As he faced Sawyer, Lan was suddenly struck by an invisible force. It was as if a wind had sprung up from nowhere and knocked him over backward.

"This is your Lower Dantian," Sawyer said. "It's your human roots as it pulls Earth energy up your legs and from your creative essence within. It can be released suddenly and strongly to push away an attacker, as well as used to regenerate your body or manifest something you need or want. But first you need to learn how to balance your mind and body within the Lower Dantian so that you can't be knocked over like I just did to you."

Sawyer showed him how to drop his mind into the Lower Dantian, then stood in front of Lan and hit him again with his Dantian energy. This time Lan stayed in place with his feet completely rooted into Earth. Lan grinned at the results but then doubted himself. "Did you send out the energy as strongly as before?" he asked.

"Stronger," Sawyer replied. Lan was startled at how a simple change with his awareness gave such an instant and powerful result.

"As you grow in your power and essence," Sawyer continued, "this energy also grows stronger. You can temporarily make it stronger with a sudden emotion such as rage or anger, but you pay a price afterward when you do. It can take days to recover."

Sawyer continued to issue warnings about the right and wrong use of the energy. "Before using this power to overwhelm an enemy, you want to control it so it doesn't act on its own. That means you control your responses when someone is physically threatening you, emotionally seducing you, or mentally trying to take your creative energy."

Sawyer showed him how to deflect the three dangers of the Lower Dantian from someone with bad intent. First, Sawyer walked toward him, physically overpowering him with his Lower Dantian energy. Lan responded in fear and tried to scramble out of the way. It made him an easy target for Sawyer to subdue. Then Sawyer demonstrated a countermove, instructing Lan to turn and walk beside Sawyer. Lan was astonished by the change that happened with that simple shift. Sawyer went from being a threatening enemy to an ally.

Sawyer continued to attempt to physically overpower Lan, including running at him with an ax over his head as if he were going to strike him. Without any weapon at all, Lan was able to pivot and run beside Sawyer, instantly shifting the energy from threatening and menacing to reassuring.

Next Sawyer showed him how to deflect someone who wanted to seduce him. At first he didn't recognize what Sawyer was doing to him. He just felt excitement and a willingness to do whatever Sawyer asked him, even when it felt a little bit dangerous. In seduction mode, Lan just wanted Sawyer's approval. This sensation was new to Lan. The only thing he could compare it to was how he felt when he saw the hawthorn tree. It was an energy that drew him in step by step. The part of his brain that normally warned him about danger seemed to shut off or even want to embrace the danger. Lan had once seen a snake seduce a mouse like that, so that it didn't run away before the snake struck. Once Lan recognized when he was being seduced, he learned to deflect it by turning the lower half of his body in a different direction, away from the seducing energy.

The final teaching with the Lower Dantian was blocking someone who was taking his creative energy. The danger had two parts...a trap and then the snap of execution. He remembered a woman in the village who used to watch him build things. When he was successful, she would go around bragging to everyone how she had shown him how to do it. He had always felt drained and powerless when she was around. Now Lan was able to see that when he felt annoyed with her bragging, she was able to reach into his Lower Dantian with an energy cord that came out of her and take his creative energy. The countermove was to simply understand the purpose behind the trap and not to respond with annoyance. He learned how to stay centered in his own Lower Dantian without reacting, no matter what trap was set.

Once Lan learned to neutralize the three dangers of the Lower Dantian, Sawyer had him switch roles. This time Lan tried to deliberately send his energy out into the space in front of him. In the beginning nothing much happened as he pushed his stomach out and scrunched up his face with his effort. Lan could see Sawyer hiding a smile as he watched him. He explained to Lan that his energy automatically responded to his mind and heart. He didn't have to learn how to send out his energy from his Lower Dantian because it happened as soon as he mentally and emotionally thought in a certain way. Lan needed to be aware of the times when his energy was trying to physically overpower, seduce or feed on someone else's creativity. Sawyer was so good at not getting caught by Lan's energy that Lan had a hard time practicing.

"Just keep observing what's happening with your energy," Sawyer encouraged him. "Once you observe it, join your mind and heart with it, then become the director of it." Lan had no idea what Sawyer was talking about so he just kept trying to observe it.

In the following days, Sawyer taught him about the Upper and Middle Dantians. The Upper Dantian, Sawyer told him, was like the branches of the trees, drawing its power from the Heavens. It was located in his forehead. The three powers of this energy seat were psychic vision, or seeing beyond walls, seeing into the future or past, and seeing through someone else's eyes. The three dangers of this energy seat involved a type of physical cutting, mental enslavement and spiritual disconnection from his essence. Avoiding these dangers centered around movement of the eyes, mouth, and sometimes hands.

The Middle Dantian was seated in his chest. Like the trunk of a tree, it drew together the energies from the Upper Dantian and the Lower Dantian. Once this was achieved, the great energy stream called the Cosmic Orbit could be turned on to circulate throughout the whole body. Lan could use this energy for increasing his power and physically healing or defending himself. He wasn't able to achieve the Cosmic Orbit yet, but Sawyer encouraged him not to worry about it and just keep practicing every day and it would turn on at some point. Until that time, it was important to know how to avoid the three energy dangers of the Middle Dantian.

The first danger was physical cruelty such as torture. Sawyer showed Lan how actually being tortured wasn't as horrifying as watching someone else being tortured in Lan's name. Lan's heart constricted in pain when Sawyer demonstrated that, even though he only pretended to torture a rock. The countermove involved bringing energy from the Lower and Upper Dantian and circulating it around his heart with his breath.

The second danger was a form of smothering that masqueraded as love and made him feel guilt and shame. To Lan it felt like being under a powerful waterfall and not being able to catch his breath. It made perfect sense the countermove would involve another breathing technique.

The third danger was becoming stuck in a negative pattern that over time would drain all the energy from his body. Lan thought back to his nights filled with the dark void and the scary beings that tried to consume him completely. He shuddered, wondering what he would have done if the pattern hadn't broken. Sawyer showed him a simple countermove. He just had to remember his true name.

Each day Lan practiced the movements, breathing techniques and energy shifts that Sawyer taught him. He also observed his own energy to better understand how it worked. Sawyer told him during an attack or in a dangerous situation, his responses had to become instinctive to effectively counter the threat.

The last skill he showed Lan was the easiest but also the most powerful—how to have quiet energy.

"Connect the energy from each of your Dantians to Gavilan above you," Sawyer instructed him.

Lan didn't understand. "What do you mean 'Gavilan above me'?" he asked. "And how do I connect the energy?"

"That part of you that you saw during the Birch Dance that holds your true name is above you. Fuse your mind and heart with each Dantian and direct it to connect to Gavilan above you."

Lan tried it and immediately felt himself get quiet. He noticed that the trees responded differently to him as though he was truly one of them. It felt restful, especially after all of the pushing and pulling he'd been doing with the other exercises. Feeling proud of how quickly he mastered that lesson and the immediate results, Lan asked Sawyer, "Does this save my energy?"

"Yes," Sawyer replied. "But asking obvious questions doesn't."

The next day Sawyer began talking to Lan about all the knowledge he had gained from the different trees.

"You have been accepted by the Forest of Dandaka as one of their own," Sawyer told him.

"How do you know that?" Lan was once again startled at what Sawyer knew about him.

"The marks you have on your body," Sawyer replied. "The night you danced with the birches was your initiation." Sawyer pulled up his tunic. He had the same marks on his stomach and back as Lan did. Lan looked at him dumbfounded, wanting to ask him so much more about the wild night of dancing, but not sure what to ask.

Sawyer didn't let him linger in the past. "The trees have given permission for you to continue to work with them when you leave the forest."

Lan's heart grew still. He knew his departure was coming, but he hadn't wanted to think about leaving Sawyer. His head said it was because he still needed to learn from him, but his heart ached at the thought of losing family again.

Sawyer handed him a set of wooden staves and gave him instructions for smoothing the sides. He next directed Lan to cut marks into each stave. The marks represented different trees. As they marked the staves, Sawyer spoke of the gifts of each tree. Oak was about strength of purpose, Alder was about renewal, and Birch was about new beginnings. Even Hawthorn was in the group. Its meaning was cleansing. Lan shuddered when he marked the stave. It would take a while, if ever, to think of Hawthorn as a friend.

"You'll have your own knowledge to add to each one," Sawyer commented. "When you work with these in divination they'll speak directly to you through your understanding of them." He told Lan he could get guidance to make a decision, see the true name of something, and find the root of a problem or situation. Sawyer reminded Lan that once he knew the true name of something, he could meld with its energy and use its gifts.

When they finished, Sawyer taught Lan how to call in the directions before doing a reading. He made Lan practice the calling until he memorized it. Lan stood in the meadow for several hours as he faced each direction and called it in.

Starting in the direction of the sunrise, he said, "I, Gavilan, call the East, the rising sun, and new beginnings. I call the winged ones and the element of air. I honor the four winds and the realm of the mind. I honor the trees of the East and their roots, branches and trunks. I choose to tell the truth without blame or judgment."

Lan pivoted a quarter turn to his right and continued, "I, Gavilan, call the South, the midday sun, and creativity. I call the element of fire and the realm of the spirit. I honor fertility, passion, and activity. I honor the land animals and insects. I honor the trees of the South and their roots, branches and trunks. I choose to show up and be present."

Once again he pivoted to his right and said, "I, Gavilan, call the West, the setting sun, and transformation. I call the element of water and the realm of the heart. I honor the animals and plants that live in water. I honor flow and receptivity. I honor the trees of the West and their roots, branches and trunks. I choose to pay attention to what has heart and meaning."

After his final turn to his right Lan said, "I, Gavilan, call the North, the eclipsed sun and the stillness between breaths. I call the element of earth and the realm of the body. I honor rocks, minerals, and crystals. I honor the trees of the North and their roots, branches and trunks. I choose to be open, not attached, to outcome."

In the beginning, Lan could only whisper the words. They felt too powerful to say in a normal voice. By the end of his practice, he was able to say the words and be in their power. Sawyer told him to pay attention to that feeling of power because it was one of the signs of melding his energy with the essence of the trees. Lan also noticed he had a strong connection to the Golden Grid. Proud that he noticed this on his own, he strutted around a little after practicing. Sawyer didn't pay him any attention.

Next, Sawyer taught him how to do different readings. He could ask a question and pick one stave. He then opened to the gifts of that particular tree and waited with a quiet mind and heart with his energy seated in his Lower Dantian. At some point, he would receive clarity on the subject. If he needed further information, he could pick another stave. Sawyer also taught him the Past, Present, and Future reading with three staves, useful for understanding the patterns that were affecting him. It reminded Lan of how he felt when he was in his Deep Thoughts, but now the process was different.

Finally, Sawyer sent him out to the middle of the meadow to do a reading on his own. Lan called in the directions and felt the surge of power and connection to the Forest of Dandaka.

He sat down on the ground and asked, "What are the Three Keys?"

Lan reached his hand into the birch container that contained the staves and picked one. It was Maple. He tried to remember what Sawyer had said about this tree and then laughed to himself when it came back to him. It actually meant keys! Quieting his mind and heart, Lan opened to the message of the Maple. Instead of spoken words, all Lan got was a vision of Sawyer. Did that mean Sawyer knew about the keys, Lan wondered? He wasn't sure.

Lan decided to try a different question, one that had been disturbing the edges of his thoughts for a while. "When do I have to leave?" Lan asked. He was afraid of the answer, but then he remembered the words for calling in North and softly repeated them under his breath. "I am open to outcome."

Lan reached into his birch container and this time pulled out Oak. Its meaning was strength of purpose. Lan was reminded of the task Boosha had given him. Connecting to the essence of Oak, Lan heard the quiet but clear word, "Soon." He knew it was true because his eyes welled up with tears.

That night after dinner Lan got out his knapsack. "Do you know anything about these things?" he asked Sawyer. Lan pulled out the Map Compass first which still wasn't working.

Sawyer took it in his hands as he felt the weight of it. "I've heard of these but I've never seen one," he said. "I know they are connected to the Balance of All That Is but that's all I know."

"Do you think it's broken?" Lan asked. "It hasn't worked since the hawthorn tree blasted me."

"Are there other times when it hasn't worked?" Sawyer asked him. Lan nodded his head, remembering the foggy pecan grove.

"Well," Sawyer ruminated, "maybe it's not just a map to show you where to go but also when to go."

"So off is stop and on is go?" Lan grinned at the simple idea.

"Possibly," Sawyer replied. Lan liked that. If it were true, he could quit worrying about when he had to leave Sawyer. Something inside of him relaxed.

Lan then held out the crystal. As before it caught the light in the room and flashed in response. Other than being beautiful to look at, Lan had no idea what it was for or what to do with it.

"Have you seen this before? Do you know anything about it?" Lan asked Sawyer.

Sawyer asked him a question in turn, "What did Boosha tell you?"

"Not much," Lan shrugged his shoulders. "She just said to give it to Asira. But I don't know who to give it to in Asira or what to tell them when I give it to them."

Sawyer ducked his head and looked into his cup of tea. He stirred it a bit and inhaled the steam.

"I've seen this before," Sawyer finally spoke. "It's part of a set. There are five of them."

Lan was puzzled. "Five of the same kind?"

"No," Sawyer replied. "Five different shapes. They are the five patterns of all life. I know that different people use them in different ways but I don't know how to use them."

Lan sighed. He was learning that asking questions just seemed to lead to more questions. Maybe this Asira place had the other four and needed this one. He put the crystal back in his rucksack and brushed the cloak with his hand. He was not going to show that to Sawyer. He knew Sawyer had seen him wearing it when he found him. Sawyer must have put it back in his rucksack but if he didn't ask anything about it, Lan wasn't going to bring it up either.

Lan squirmed a bit in his seat. He wasn't quite sure how to ask the next question. "Boosha told me to take the crystal and the Three Keys and deliver them to Asira," Lan said. "But I don't have any keys. I don't know what she meant by that part so I'm not going to be able to do it." Lan felt the familiar words rise up inside of him, "I can't do it! Don't ask me!" but pushed them back down.

Sawyer didn't respond right away but threw another log on the fire and poked the half-burned ends that had fallen out back toward the hot middle. Lan began to wonder from Sawyer's silence if maybe he hadn't spoken the words out loud.

Instead, Sawyer asked, "Did Boosha say anything to you about initiations?"

"Yeah, she said she hadn't given me my third initiation yet," Lan told him, remembering that frightening last day, the last moment really, that they were together.

Sawyer paused, then took a deep breath. "I've got some good news and some not so good news. The good news is I can tell you about the keys. The bad news is you're missing one of them and I don't know how to fix that." Sawyer held up his hand as Lan started to rise out of his chair, his energy from his Dantians spraying into the room with his alarm and agitation. Sawyer waited while Lan reseated himself in his Lower Dantian and got quiet with his energy again.

"The Three Keys are part of the Balance of All That Is." Sawyer paused, then corrected himself. "Well, they are part of it, but they are like helpers, too."

As Sawyer talked, Lan observed he was checking the Golden Grid periodically to make sure he was using the right words. At least that's what he seemed to be doing. "All life must grow," Sawyer continued. "The Three Keys make sure life stays in harmony and balance as it grows. It's like a recipe that has to be followed step by step. Step one, the First Key, is called The Opening. It's when all the forces pull together to begin a new pattern of growth. You feel it when you're starting or beginning something you've never done before. There's a sense of anticipation like when you know something good is about to happen."

Lan immediately flashed back to his excitement when he was in the rock pool and decided to continue the journey Boosha had sent him on.

Sawyer nodded as if Lan had spoken, then continued, "The Second Key is called The Chaos. It's when everything goes back to pure essence before form. It's like when a caterpillar becomes soupy mush inside his chrysalis as he changes from worm to butterfly. It can be a time of confusion or disorder, because what was ordered falls away."

Lan thought about his last days in the forest when all of the tree energy had gone dormant in the roots. And then he'd experienced the hawthorn tree. He grimaced. That was not a fun time.

Again, as if he heard Lan's thoughts, Sawyer continued, "Some people love this key. They use a special form of Magick at this time to manifest what they want.

"The final or Third Key is called The Mastery," Sawyer continued, "It's when growth reaches a higher level. When that happens you have new levels of gifts and power you can use in the world."

Lan thought about his time here with Sawyer and how much he'd grown in his power. But then a question popped into his mind. "So who has the Three Keys?" Lan asked.

"Technically everyone," Sawyer replied. "But in the time before the Great Shift, the Balance of All That Is was almost destroyed and the Three Keys went dormant. Only a few people kept them alive within. Those people are called The Awakeners. That's because when they use their Three Keys, they awaken someone else's Three Keys as well."

"So was Boosha an Awakener?" Lan asked.

"Yes, Sawyer replied. "But she only had time to awaken two of the keys within you. I'm not an Awakener so I don't know how you'll get the Third Key."

With this news Lan fell into a deep hopelessness. There was so much he still didn't understand! In fact, it seemed he didn't understand anything at all. The life as he had known it back in the village with Boosha was completely different from his life now. He had felt safe in the daily rituals of the village. He knew exactly what was going to happen each day and through the seasons. Like the last of the leaves being torn off the trees in the winter, his old life was all gone. Completely overwhelmed, Lan didn't notice he'd once again fallen out of balance. He crawled into bed and pulled the cover over his head.

That night Lan had a disturbing dream. He looked at the double full moons in the night sky. His heart was full of love for the beauty of the two moons that danced in the heavens. One of the moons was slightly behind the other. Together they looked like a side-lying figure 8. As Lan stood in the clearing, connecting to the full moons through the Golden Grid, his heart opened wider and wider. His body filled with the power of knowing his purpose and what he needed to do on his journey. All the pieces fell into place and he felt his mind beginning to light up with the knowing of it all. Suddenly a strange object shot into the sky, heading for the moons. It hit the first one and exploded it into many pieces. The second moon spun off into the darkness away from Earth.

In his dream, Lan fell to his knees in grief. His first thought was how much he'd miss seeing the moons at night. As if they'd been his parents watching over him, they had been his night-time companions throughout his whole life. Then the Earth began shaking and quaking beneath him. He fell into dread and despair as he knew this was the end, forever, of The Balance of All That Is.

CHAPTER EIGHT

WHAT THE FIREBIRD KNEW

Asira stood on top of the bluff looking at the world below her. The village was miniature, looking perfect from this perspective. She could see people, but they looked more like ants. Strange to think she liked ants better than people. The flow of the river couldn't be seen from her perch. The rapids looked frozen like the wings of hair at the Director's temples who she couldn't stand.

The only movement that Asira could make out was in the Forest of Dandaka. It was odd, though. Normally, a windy day didn't set the trees in motion. It was as though the forest created its own weather. Now something moved through the trees like a weird sky snake. Often there would be an explosion of birds when the movement stopped. Takaani was watching the strange movement, too, with his head cocked to one side. "What do you think that is?" she asked him. Instead of an answer, Takaani just bent his head and licked his paw.

Almost every day, Asira came to the bluff, scanning the forest for the arrival of the young man in the blue cloak. It had been four moon months since she'd had her fire vision and changed her mind about exiting by floating off the waterfall. It was now Alder Moon and the Day Out of Balance was upon them. It was also the end of winter.

Asira was beginning to doubt what she'd seen in the fire that night. Maybe it had just been a dream instead of a vision. She knew that the coming month would bring more visitors to Our Place. It was the start of spring, and mountain passes would soon open. The river would soon be safe again for travel after the biggest runoff from snowmelt subsided.

Asira shifted restlessly. Last night she'd watched the river Urubamba glow with blue light under the Double Moons. It didn't always happen on this Day Out of Balance, but when it did it was beautiful to watch. The special algae was usually a sign of an earlier than usual spring. She felt torn in conflict, part of her wanting to leave before all the travelers started arriving, part of her wanting to stay longer with her family. When she left, it would be a forever goodbye.

She wasn't sure how much longer she could wait for the person from her vision to show up. With a sudden toss of her hair and straightening of her shoulders, she pivoted away from the bluff. She'd leave by herself if he didn't come soon. Her plan was to carefully plant a story about leaving to gather certain healing herbs. It would take her away from Our Place for several weeks. When Asira didn't return, hopefully Kuut would just assume something had happened to her and wouldn't take it out on her family.

Asira wasn't sure how Kuut knew when someone was arriving or what they wanted to barter, but somehow he always knew. By observing the traps that people began putting out for animals, or when there was a burst of new activity in the midden as people looked for objects they could trade or sell, she recognized more visitors were arriving.

Asira still visited the traps and released any animals that were caught. She had to be careful to make it look like an accidental escape. She wondered what would happen to all of the animals when she was gone. Maybe she could teach Susie how to release them.

Now Asira trotted off to check the traps. The first five held nothing, but the next one was a Firebird trap. From a distance she saw the flash of bright red and her heart sank. People rarely trapped these birds because they were so observant and smart. They also didn't survive for long after being trapped.

She saw a Firebird lying on his side as she approached. At first Asira feared he was dead because he lay so still. Then she caught the faint movement of breath underneath his brilliant orange and red plumage. Asira told Takaani to stay at a safe distance, then approached, stepping carefully on rocks to avoid leaving a sign of any footprints. Opening the trap, she gently took out the Firebird and wrapped him in her overcoat. She reset the trap, but in a way that disabled it if another Firebird got too close. From a distance it looked normal. Perhaps the person who set the trap wouldn't discover it wasn't operating.

As quickly as possible without drawing any attention to herself, Asira took the Firebird back to her home. There she began to work on him with her healing powers. When the Firebird was able to lift his head, she spooned a little water into his beak. Over the coming days, the Firebird slowly recovered his ability to walk. With his wing broken from the trap, flying was going to take longer.

One day, Asira heard, "Thank you," in her mind accompanied with a vision of the Firebird bowing his head to her. His bright, inquisitive eyes began to watch her when she was healing other animals or working with her herbs. After she tied up his broken wing so he could walk better and not reinjure it, he began following her as she went on her rounds. At first he rode on Takaani's back for longer distances, but soon he was able to keep up on his own. Takaani looked relieved not to have a bright red ornament on his shoulders.

Asira wondered if the Firebird had any wisdom to share with her or even information from his flights. She respected his healing space and stayed quiet, enjoying the gentle bond of energy between them. At times she felt him observing the darkness of despair she carried within her, but he left her alone about it. She found it a relief not to have to hide that part of herself, pretending it didn't exist or that it was wrong.

The next day she went down to the river Urubamba to collect some special plants that grew on the banks that time of year. This part of the river was closer to the falls and the normally flat surface was crisscrossed with currents. It was almost as though the river knew what was coming and was getting ready. She watched the currents, entranced by their different patterns. The Firebird, who she'd started referring to as Sparky, stood beside her. Asira was still startled as to how tall he stood, reaching above her knees, and how broad his wingspan was when they were fully stretched out.

Sparky broke the quiet energy of companionship between them and for the first time began communicating with Asira in picture words. "The river flows like the air," he said. Asira saw a picture of him high in the sky, floating on the air. It reminded her of her favorite sport of water gliding, arms out-stretched, face to the sky.

"Don't worry," she told him. "You'll be back in the air again and probably very soon. Your wing is much stronger now."

Responding to her encouraging words with just a nod of his head, Sparky stayed intent on his lesson. "I want to tell you about the spirals." He brought her attention to the beautiful circular pattern of the swirling water. "The first is a double spiral, moving up from the bottom of the river, while another spiral from the surface moves down to the bottom. You can find these spirals within all living things. Tend to these spirals in your healing work with animals." Sparky lightly touched her knees with his good wing, inviting her to feel the upward spiral. Then he touched her upper back, inviting her to feel the downward spiral. Asira was slightly bemused by the sudden outpouring of information from Sparky after days of quiet companionship.

"When you work with someone who is physically weak and want them to become stronger, you help them with the upward spiral. And when you work with someone who is emotionally weak or has sustained a big shock, you enhance the downward spiral."

Because Sparky was showing her as well as telling her, Asira experienced what he was talking about. She felt herself grow stronger and the darkness within her shrank. When she thought about those people or situations when she felt helpless, they didn't seem as scary or as overwhelming to her. Asira bounced up and down with excitement. No one had ever taught her about healing before. Maybe practicing this before any of her healings would help her with the dizziness she experienced.

On a different day, they walked down to a particularly wild part of the river. "There," said Sparky, pointing with his wing to the middle of the river. "Do you see the triple spiral?"

Asira squinted but couldn't see what he was talking about. Looking down, she saw that Sparky was drawing something in the dirt. When he stepped back she saw the triple spiral he was talking about. "Trace that with your finger," Sparky told her.

As Asira traced the triple spiral, she realized that it was one continuous line from start to finish. She felt a gentle rocking within her, soothing and comforting. Sparky nodded his head at her discovery. "This is the way energy should move through healthy air or water. Since each body is made up mostly of air like me or water like you, this spiral needs to be present for health." Now when Asira looked at the river she could see the triple spiral and knew it was the signal of healthy and healing water.

"If you lose this spiral within you, you can come to water and lay in it. Or you can stand by running water and connect your inner triple spiral to the water like we are talking about right now. It removes anything that might make you sick if you drink it. It's the same when you are working with animals or people."

At the mention of healing people, Asira shuddered, but the thought wasn't as uncomfortable as she'd felt in the past.

The next day, Sparky told her he needed to show her one more spiral. He called it the Golden Spiral. As they walked down to a different part of the river, he began telling her about the importance of the Golden Spiral and the Three Keys. "What are the Three Keys?" she asked.

Suddenly there was a shout behind her. Looking back, she saw a man pointing to them and yelling to someone else. "Quickly!" Sparky commanded. "Untie my wing. I must leave now"

As Asira untied the sling with trembling fingers, she protested, "You aren't ready to fly yet."

"Oh yes I am," said Sparky. "I'll use the double spiral currents of the air to be stronger and fly faster." With that, he sprang into the air and began to fly, slowly at first until he caught a spiral of air over the river. Asira watched him in awe as he quickly flew upward hardly using his wings at all.

Three people thundered up beside her and one grabbed her by the arm. "You better explain yourself to Kuut," he demanded. He pulled her roughly toward the town, yanking on her arm when she pulled back. Asira didn't want to stop watching Sparky as he glided and spiraled through the air. Her heart ached at the rapid parting, but then soared in joy at his freedom and escape.

Dragging her into the center of the town, her captor yelled for the Director. Kuut came strolling out of his house, rubbing his eyes and then running his fingers through his hair. It was obvious he'd been sleeping even though it was almost noon.

"There better be a good reason you are waking me up," he growled.

"Oh there is," responded the man who still held onto Asira's arm. "I found her down by the river with a Firebird. It looked like she was helping it to escape, not trying to catch it."

"Is this true?" Kuut looked at her in amusement.

Asira knew she couldn't answer completely. "Yes and no," she hedged.

Kuut's demeanor changed from amused tolerance to anger. "What in the blazes does that mean? How dare you speak so insolently to me?" He took a menacing step toward her raising his arm to strike her.

Beside her, Takaani growled low in his throat.

"Did that mangy wolf just threaten me?" Kuut said, turning his hard gaze toward the animal. Silently, Asira sent a message to Takaani, "Go!" She repeated it with more urgency and showed him she'd be all right. Takaani turned and trotted toward their home.

"I'm so sorry," Asira said trying to placate the Director, whose arm was still in the air. "He misunderstood you when you raised your arm. He thought you wanted to strike me."

Kuut muttered something under his breath and then made a

gesture with his hand as if he was smoothing down his hair. "Of course, I don't want to hurt you. Now explain to me what you meant."

"I found the Firebird a few days back, with a broken wing," Asira explained. "I knew he wasn't worth anything with a broken wing so I started to heal it. I was just having the bird give its wing a try when your men came upon me. I had no intention of letting the bird go and tied a string around his foot, but your men startled me and I dropped the string."

"Hmmm," Kuut looked at her, trying to determine if she was lying. Asira looked back at him with wide eyes, not showing fear or worry. Inside, she ran her two spirals of energy upward and downward to make herself stronger physically and emotionally, without trembling as she would have in the past.

"Well, all right then," the Director finally said. "But if I ever see that mongrel again, I will have him captured and killed immediately. Now get out of here."

Asira ran to her family's home, ready to burst into tears. Her beloved Takaani was now in horrible danger. She didn't stop until she fell into the arms of Karen, her mother. Then the sobs came pouring out as her mother tried to calm her and find out what had happened at the same time.

Just then her father, Ryan, hurried in. "I've heard the whole story," he said. "When we have a chance, I want to hear everything about the Firebird, but first we need to make sure Takaani is safe."

Hiccupping, after her crying jag, Asira said, "But what can we do?"

"I was afraid this day was going to come," Ryan responded, "And I came up with a plan. I think we need to take Takaani up to a dome cave I found at the base of Mount Ausungate. We'll take more supplies with us. If the day comes you have to leave, you'll have a place to go."

Asira was still too numb from the scare and her hysterical sobbing to take it all in, but nodded her head slowly.

"It's a couple of days from here so let's pack up and get going."

As they quietly left Our Place with multiple packs and Takaani at their heels, Asira's somber mood gradually changed to one of lightness. The town had always been a place of tension and stress where she had to hide her true nature. Being out on the trail with the wide-open spaces all around her was exhilarating. No one was watching her every move or scowling at her. She felt a shadow pass over her. Looking up, she realized they were being followed by Sparky.

She sent up a silent "Hello, are you okay?" to him while pointing him out to her dad. "Look, there's the Firebird I helped heal." Sparky waggled his wings in reply, then flew a few spirals overhead.

They covered the miles at an easy pace for the rest of the day, as Asira shared her adventures in healing and the lessons Sparky had taught her. Her father listened in wonder as she talked about her gifts of healing as if they were the same as breathing and drinking. Her power and beauty sparkled in the air with each word she uttered. He couldn't have been prouder of her if she'd been his actual daughter.

At the end of the second day of hiking, they reached the foothills of Ausungate, the majestic peak that towered above Our Place.

"Not too far now," Ryan said to Asira.

Behind an initial stand of pines, they approached an area of towering rocks that sprung up from the ground in individual groupings. Skirting around the edge of a rock cluster, Ryan motioned to Asira to follow him, then he disappeared right in front of her. Blinking at this sudden act of magic, Asira approached the spot where she's last seen him. A hand reached out from a crack in the rock and pulled her into a small opening. Takaani followed her closely. Winding through a narrow opening that was tight even for Asira, they eventually popped into the hidden dome. A lovely grassy area opened in front of them. In one corner, a spring bubbled with water, while in another an outcropping of rock made a natural shelter. With the towering rocks encircling them but open to the sky it was like a house with no roof.

Asira and Ryan began to build a bed for Takaani, who watched them anxiously. He knew that he was going to be separated from Asira. "Do you think he'll stay here?" she asked Ryan.

"Yes, if you leave one of your pieces of clothing for him to lie on and tell him to wait for you. He'll hunt on his own and come back here each night."

Asira hoped that was true, because the idea of him showing up in the village scared her.

Ryan continued. "You'll be back here in three or four weeks."

Asira asked how he could be so sure. Ryan looked at her with a smile on his face. "Did you think I didn't know what you've been planning? You're going to go look for your real parents, right?"

Asira's mouth dropped open. She thought she'd been doing such a good job hiding her plan from Ryan and Karen. She didn't want them to think she didn't love and appreciate them, or thought of them as anything but her parents. She didn't even remember her actual parents and couldn't imagine them taking better care of her or loving her more than Ryan and Karen had.

Ryan looked at her with soft eyes. "I know you can't stay another season with visitors who are coming for healing. Your mom thinks you'll get better at it, but I know how hard it is for you. I asked myself what would I do in that situation and I thought...I'd go look for my real parents. It was just a guess, but a good one by the look on your face!"

"Do you know where they are?" Asira asked him.

Ryan shook his head. "No. I only know that they went up into the mountains. It's whispered that there are towns up there where those who want to stay hidden from prying eyes go."

Asira became excited with that information. "So maybe the guy who's coming to help me is going to help me look for them!"

Ryan looked at her like she'd eaten a bad mushroom. "What are you talking about? What guy? Do I know him?"

Ducking her head, Asira kicked the dirt. She'd forgotten they didn't know about her vision. Haltingly, Asira told him about the night of the fire without telling Ryan what she'd planned on doing. It was hard to explain how she "knew" things, like how the guy with the blue cloak that she'd seen in her fire was coming to help her, when they hadn't actually talked. But when he'd turned and looked into her eyes, she just knew. It was after that vision the idea to look for her actual parents sprouted like a sunflower in the field of her mind. Maybe her parents could explain what was wrong with her, or how this healing gift worked. Maybe one of them was a healer, too.

Ryan didn't know what to think about the vision. There was much about his daughter he didn't understand, but he did know she needed to leave the village. Her situation would only become more dangerous with the arrival of more visitors. Looking for her parents would give Asira a plan to move forward, instead of just running from her past.

After the long day and intense conversation, Ryan and Asira fell silent as they made camp for the night. He showed her how to build a fire under the branches of a tree so the smoke couldn't be seen by others. The trick was to keep the fire small and make sure to put it out completely before sleeping. Asira slept next to Takaani to enjoy his company on their last night for a while. She didn't let her thoughts stray into "What if" this was their last time together. A month was a long time and a lot could happen.

The next day Asira hugged Takaani and sent him the picture message to wait for her here and not follow her back to the village. Leaving some food for him, she showed him it was okay to go out hunting when he got hungry, but not to let himself be seen by anyone. Finally, she left one of her old shirts for him to use as a bed.

Just before leaving the secret crevasse, she turned and looked at him. Her last view of Takaani was of him sitting by her shirt, wagging his tail in the dirt. He was so trusting of her! She would go back to the village and immediately begin preparing her own departure. With or without the guy from the fire, she was going to be back here in a month or less.

After returning to the village and slipping in quietly so that no one noticed they'd been gone, Ryan and Asira resumed their daily routines. She began collecting and drying the healing plants that she'd take with her. Karen, her mom, brought her another set of clothes to take with her while Ryan finished a new carryall that could almost hold everything she needed. He came back a few days later with another pack. It was for Takaani! Asira wasn't sure how Takaani would like it, but she had to admit it was a good idea.

One day she climbed up to the top of the bluff to look out over the forest one last time. Scanning up and down the river, she saw no one. As she stood there, hoping that this time someone would show up or she'd see a flash of blue, a shadow swooped over her. She looked up, delighted to see Sparky. She hadn't realized how much she'd missed her companion. Sparky told her about a trap that had caught more animals, this time some of the mountain ponies.

Following Sparky as he flew, Asira hurried toward the mountains. In a little ravine, a trap corral had been set. Inside five mountain ponies were neighing and pawing up the grass-covered dirt. Asira knew she didn't have much time before whoever had set the trap came to get them. Running down the slope of the ravine, she grabbed the main pole-gate blocking the ponies' escape and pulled it slightly open. If the ponies pushed their way out, it would look like they'd naturally escaped.

Moving back up the ravine more carefully then she had come down, Asira stepped on rocks and trees to cover her tracks. Soon she heard the ponies' hooves thundering behind her as they discovered the opening and rushed out. As she gained the top of the ravine, she turned and saw the ponies on the other side. They'd all stopped and were looking toward her. Bowing their heads toward her, she heard floating across the wind, "Thank you." Asira raised her hand in farewell, then watched them as they turned and galloped toward the mountain with flying manes and tails.

The next week Asira kept busy releasing animals from traps. Each day Sparky showed her where to go. There seemed to be more of them now and she knew that the villagers were getting ready to start trading again with the visitors.

One day Sparky flew over her and signaled her to follow him. Thinking he had found another trapped animal, Asira grabbed her pack of healing plants and followed. Instead of a trap, he took her to the midden. Normally she only came here when she needed a container to hold her supplies. Thinking there was an animal hurt somewhere down in the heaped piles of rusty metal and broken glass, she slipped over the edge and cautiously picked her way down and then through the piles of discarded material. Sparky was ahead of her, circling over one area. When she arrived, she couldn't see any animal.

Stopping, she sent a question up to Sparky, then cocked her head to listen for any cries of distress. Nothing.

Asira looked up at Sparky. Why was she here? Sparky was flying in spirals in response to her question. He dove down toward a pile of rubbish, then veered off at the last second. Walking over to where Sparky had swooped down, she saw light shoot out from underneath a pile of trash. Asira dug through the rubbish and discovered a beautiful crystal. Iridescent light shot from it, then it was neutral. It had very little dirt on it, which amazed Asira. Had it been lying there for a long time? It looked so out of place with all the decaying discards around it. Asira felt compelled to pick it up and hold it. It was the size of her palm and had many facets, all of them triangles. The crystal looked clear unless she gazed into its middle at just the right angle and then she saw the pearly swirl of light again.

"Crystalline Emotion," she heard from above. Asira had been so entranced at the sight of it she'd forgotten Sparky for a moment.

"What does that mean?" she whispered.

"That's its name. Take it with you when you go."

Startled, Asira wondered if everyone knew her plans. Her other questions about the crystal flew out of her mind as her brow wrinkled in worry. Tucking the crystal into her herb bag, she carefully picked her way out of the midden. She felt a sudden urgency, but couldn't move fast until she climbed out of the trash pile.

"That's it!" she thought. "I'm packing and leaving tomorrow before one more person finds out my plans." Asira felt a deep yearning to see Takaani again. Something inside of her broke free at her decision and she almost felt like she could fly up to Sparky.

Deciding to say goodbye to her family that night, Asira headed back to her little home to finish packing. Habit made her swerve one last time and head to the bluff to see if anyone had arrived from the Forest of Dandaka. She expected it to be just like all the other times she'd looked, and wouldn't see anyone. This time, a lone figure stood on the opposite side of the river. Her heart lifted at the sight of him, but then dropped. He wasn't wearing a blue cloak. She watched him for a little bit, wondering who he was and if he was just the first of the next wave of visitors. He seemed to be searching for a way to cross the river.

Asira made a small "humph" sound under her breath. Why was she waiting for someone to save her? She was finally ready to admit it. That vision had just been a dream after all. It had served its purpose and she was still here on the planet.

In a few days, she would start the journey to look for her other parents. She had Takaani and herself. That's all she needed.

CHAPTER NINE

THE BADLANDS

Lan woke gasping for air, still locked into the dream of the moons blowing up and the Earth shaking apart. He actually felt the pain of the Golden Grid tearing and he realized that in his dream a Dark Grid had taken its place.

Rising, he went outside. The night air was cool on his feverish face. He worked on reseating his energy through the Dantian exercises Sawyer had shown him. After a while he felt calmer. He was afraid to look up at the double moons, though. He stood with his head down and eyes closed.

Sawyer's voice floated out to him from the dark. "There was a time when there was only one moon."

Startled out of his focused centering, Lan lifted his head and looked for Sawyer. He stood at the side of the clearing. As always, Sawyer's energy was quiet, making it hard for Lan to locate him in the dark. Lan walked toward him, his agitation surfacing again. He opened his mouth, then shut it, preferring to wait and see what Sawyer was going to say. For once, he wouldn't ask a stupid question.

"Just before the Great Shift when the world fell out of The

Balance of All That Is," Sawyer continued, talking softly, "a group of scientists tried to restore the balance by placing a second moon behind the first. The Double Moons were able to slow down the coming of the Great Shift and the Earth from falling apart completely, but they didn't totally restore The Balance of All That Is."

Lan felt himself fall into the familiar confusion that came with Sawyer's stories. They only seemed to open up new questions when what he really wanted was simply an explanation of his dream.

"The Double Moons," Sawyer continued in his soft voice, "brought in a temporary balance most of the time so that the Golden Grid could be repaired. But as in all things about balance, there are certain times of the year when the Double Moons bring out all that isn't in balance with the Three Keys. You must learn those times of the year and take extra caution."

Lan had to stop him at this point. "Why didn't we know these things in our village?"

"Because on the other side of the Forest of Dandaka," Sawyer replied, "the Golden Grid has been fully repaired. But there are forces that want to stop that from happening everywhere. Those forces want to bring in the Dark Grid instead."

Lan quivered deep in his belly. That was exactly what he had seen in his dream!

"Pay attention," Sawyer said, bringing Lan back to the stillness of the night and the clearing. "You must learn these dates so you can protect yourself. We are nearly at the second one of the year which is why you had the bad dream."

Lan scanned his inner calendar based on his sense of natural time. He knew that they were in Alder Moon and that the first day of the Vernal Equinox was almost here. He had been with Sawyer for almost three months.

Sawyer again read Lan's thoughts and nodded in confirmation, although in the dark Lan could barely see the movement. "There are eight days called the Days Out of Balance. These days call forth those lifeforms that are not connected to the Golden Grid or the Three Keys. If you had your Third Key you'd be able to fight them, but for now you just have to get out of the way."

Lan didn't hear what Sawyer said after he heard him mention lifeforms. His mind filled with picture-feelings as he saw strange plants and animals that overcame him with dread.

Sawyer's voice took on urgency and he began talking faster. "The first Day Out of Balance falls on the new moon during the Hawthorn Moon. You were still too ill to notice, but I almost lost you on that one. The dark forces were very potent then."

"Now, the second one is arriving tomorrow. What might happen, I'm not sure. But there's been a disturbance in the Golden Gird that is growing louder. No matter what happens the best solution is to be as quiet with your energy as possible. Don't attract attention to yourself."

Sawyer continued talking, his voice low but still intense. He told Lan the other six dates of the Days Out of Balance. Although no one was ever certain what would happen on those dates, there were certain themes to watch for and possible ways to stay protected. Sawyer explained he needed to pay attention to an approaching date and avoid being out in the open.

Lan wanted to know more about the images he was seeing in his mind. "What are these lifeforms not connected to the Golden Grid?" he asked. "Where did they come from?"

Sawyer felt the urgency to keep preparing for the day ahead, but he took a moment to explain. "In the days before the Great Shift," he said, "there were many scientists experimenting with different lifeforms. They called it bioengineering. Some of their intentions were good as they tried to solve problems for the planetary changes that were happening. Many animals were disappearing completely and these scientists were trying to help them avoid extinction. But there were other scientists who had a different agenda. These scientists were pretending to invent positive solutions but what they really wanted was to break the Balance of All That Is and take over the source of life itself."

Lan shuddered again with the picture-feelings in his mind. He saw men working in hidden places doing despicable things to animals as they cut and sliced their very essence and added other elements. Others did the same thing to trees and other plants.

Sawyer told him, "That feeling of revulsion that you are experiencing is how you know you are looking at a lifeform that has been altered in that way. Unfortunately, those lifeforms are desperate to connect to the grid of life for energy and think that the only way to get it is by destroying other lifeforms."

Lan was so deeply entrenched in the conversation he barely noticed the darkness had shifted to the lighter tones of dawn. Sawyer glanced around him, stood and stretched. "Come," he said. "We must prepare to leave."

Walking back to the cottage that had been his home for almost three months, Lan felt a brief moment of sadness that they were leaving, but that sorrow was soon replaced with excitement. It was time to finish the journey Boosha had sent him on. He felt ready and doubly so if Sawyer was going to go with him.

"I hope to come with you," Sawyer confirmed. "But there are things that we don't know about yet that may prevent that from happening. Your journey to Asira may not be the end, but perhaps a beginning. Always follow the Map Compass and if we get separated, know that we will meet up again."

Lan puzzled over Sawyer's words as he repacked his rucksack but then concentrated on adding to his pack all the new things he'd made. Besides his cloak, crystal, and Map Compass, he added a dozen pine pitch sticks, a good supply of cordage and his bow and quiver of arrows. Finally he tucked in the birch box with his Tree Staves. Sawyer then handed him a dozen cakes of his special flat bread made from chestnuts and pecan flour and sweetened with a little bit of maple syrup. Lan watched Sawyer out of the corner of his eye as Sawyer packed his own tools and supplies. He moved with a smooth efficiency that belied his urgency.

Suddenly Sawyer went still. Dropping to all fours, he placed his ear on the ground. "Hellkite!" he cursed. "They are coming. We've run out of time."

Sawyer grabbed Lan's arm. "Listen to me. We're going to have to separate. I will lead them away."

Who was coming? Lan looked across the clearing toward the forest. Trees were swaying and cracking loudly as they broke and crashed down. Seven enormous animals broke through and thundered abruptly into the clearing. Lan froze at the sight of them, his fear mixed with revulsion. Their large heads had reddish eyes and two vicious-looking tusks covered in vines and broken branches. They had long trunks that they used to grasp small trees and pull them out of the ground. Covered with thick, matted hair, these animals smelled foul from clear across the meadow.

Lan whispered to Sawyer, "What are they?"

Suddenly, they spotted Lan and Sawyer. Turning, they thundered across the meadow toward them. Sawyer yelled at him as he veered away from Lan and sprinted toward the forest behind the cottage, "They're Mammophants. I'll draw them away. Check your Map Compass!"

It was clear the Mammophants had spotted Sawyer as he ran toward the trees. They tore after him in pursuit. But one of the animals locked eyes with Lan and veered toward him. Lan felt his energy go quiet as if a blanket had been thrown over him. The Mammophant stopped looking at Lan, changing the angle of his charge. Still, he passed by so closely that Lan felt the brush of its spiky hair across his face. Three of them crashed through the cottage as if it was only made of air. Then they were gone as they hurtled into the forest after Sawyer.

Lan stood shocked, his mind completely blank. In a blink, everything was gone. One minute he'd been talking with Sawyer inside the home that had been his haven for three months and the next moment it lay flattened, in ruins. The only thing he could remember was Sawyer shouting at him to check the Map Compass. With shaky hands, he fumbled opened his rucksack and took it out. Sure enough, it was working again. A wave of resentment and sadness rose up within him. Why couldn't it have started working yesterday?

Lan crossed the clearing in the direction the Mammophants had come and, with one last look behind him at the wrecked cottage, entered the forest. His journey had started again.

Back on the Map Compass path, Lan walked in a daze the first several days after the Day Out of Balance. He felt as if he'd fallen back in time to the day he'd first left the village. All that he'd learned and the confidence he'd gained had disappeared. Once again, he was on a journey that seemed to be something only he could complete. Once again, he was worried about a beloved member of his adopted family. Worst of all, once again he was alone. Was he cursed to always have his family ripped away from him?

Slowly the events of that strange day receded and with it his brooding. With the smells of dirt and the different trees, Lan instinctively connected to the Golden Grid again. He noticed that when he was connected, his loneliness disappeared. When he started to miss Sawyer, he clung to his final words. They'd meet up again. Just as he knew with every fiber of his being that he would return to Boosha someday, he knew he'd reconnect with Sawyer. Their time together was not over.

Checking the Map Compass, Lan began calculating how long it would take him to get to Asira. He was just a little over half way there. It had taken him two and a half months to get to this point, so he figured he had two more months to go. Luckily the days were getting longer and warmer. He could put in more hours walking during the day and less hours building shelter and fires.

Lan wondered how fast he could move through the forest without tiring out the next day. He tried picking up his pace, walking faster, but ultimately it put too much stress on his feet. Then he alternated running with walking. Instead of helping him, he seemed to make less progress. His hunger increased and he spent too much time searching for food.

One morning he woke up with an idea. What if he used the movements that Sawyer had taught him? He began simply standing tall and bringing his awareness into his three Dantians. He brought energy into his Lower Dantian as if he were a tree with roots deep in the ground. Lan quieted his mind by softening his gaze and centering in the middle of his head, open to the sun above him. Lan decided to experiment with the Middle Dantian. He connected it to the other Dantians and felt a small current of energy circulating through his body. It seemed to charge him and helped him walk further and recover from his tiredness more quickly. Was this the Cosmic Orbit Sawyer had told him about?

Wondering if he could speed up that inner flow, Lan tried changing his breathing, the length of his stride and the best foot placement. One day he noticed that if he leaned from his ankles, the circular flow within him felt stronger and faster. He let his body fall forward and his legs catch him. Now Lan experimented with different speeds of moving again. This time when he ran, he didn't tire or get extra hungry. If he kept his feet beneath him and his stride short, he could run for hours. The dot that represented him on the Map Compass began to show dramatic progress.

Lan fell into a rhythm—running during the day, stopping at night, eating, sleeping, waking, eating and then back on the trail, moving again. There were some nights when his mind refused to be quiet and began circling around the same questions. He had two of the three keys but how was he going to get the third? And how was he going to deliver those to the people of Asira? He missed his nightly talks with Sawyer, who didn't have all the answers, but had so much wisdom to share with him. With Sawyer, the missing gaps of his knowledge were just openings for new learning. Alone, these gaps threw him into doubt, and he wondered if he could finish what Boosha had asked him to do. It was so clear to him that he wasn't the right one for this task...why had Boosha insisted he do it?

One night, Lan stopped on the edge of a small clearing. The weather had been so mild he could just sleep in his cloak without building a fire. He liked sleeping against trees with curved trunks that fit his back. At the first hint of light, he checked the Map Compass and then was on his feet and running again. Today was different. The Map Compass had stopped working. Lan felt himself fall into the familiar frustration. His thoughts circled gloomily as he wondered how long the Map Compass would refuse to work. Would it be days? Or even months, like when he was with Sawyer?

Lan's thoughts circled chaotically until he remembered to work with his Dantians. He brought all his agitated energy back in and seated himself in the three centers. He breathed into each one. Perhaps he was supposed to receive a message through the Golden Grid and he needed to be still, centered and open.

As the sun rose in the small clearing, his eyes were drawn to a large bush with leaves of brilliant, cobalt blue. He'd never seen a blue bush before. It mesmerized him. Then he noticed that the leaves were moving, even though there was no breeze. Lan squinted his eyes just slightly, then decided to get closer to examine this amazing sight.

Just as he began to stand, one of the leaves detached itself and seemed to float into the air. More and more leaves did the same. Suddenly it dawned on Lan. He was watching butterflies! His heart opened in wonder and he remembered looking at butterflies with Boosha. Lan wished with all his heart that she were here now to share this with him. He wanted to get up and dance with the butterflies in the morning light. Then he held his breath as he saw one approaching him. Maybe it would land on his hand.

Before he could put out his hand, the blue butterfly floated up to him and landed right on his belly button. Lan felt his Lower Dantian explode open. His external awareness of his surroundings disappeared as his inner senses began to shimmer and radiate light. He felt like he'd stepped into the middle of the Empowerment Crystal.

Entranced by all the swirling colors within his mind and the indescribable feelings of his body, Lan only faintly heard the words, "This is your third initiation."

Immediately he was swept back in time and he was nine years old. He and Boosha were standing in the forest looking for plants. "Come here, boy," Boosha said to him. He obeyed, only reaching her shoulders when he stood beside her. She touched his forehead and Lan fell into a trance. He faintly heard her whisper the words, "May you honor the innate wisdom within all life."

After that, Lan lost all sense of time and place. He slowly came back into awareness of his surroundings, thinking how strange it was that the sun was almost setting. He'd had no sense of time passing. When Lan sharply inhaled to ask a question, Boosha shushed him by placing a finger on his lips.

She leaned down and said, "That was The Opening, the First Key."

Now Lan saw himself and Boosha in another place in the forest. They were gathering sweet berries for a cake that Boosha planned to make for his birthday celebration. This time when she called him over, he was level with her head. She touched his heart and again he fell into a trance. He heard her whispering words that didn't make any sense to him. "May you remember, honor, and protect your gifts."

This time Lan heard a sound that started deep in his bones, then came pouring out of his chest. He cocked his head to listen. How odd that he knew this sound with every fiber of his being but had never heard it before. He felt empowered to the depth of his being as strange geometric shapes flashed through his mind. When he became aware of his surroundings again, Boosha told him, "That was The Chaos, the Second Key."

As these scenes faded from his memory, he was drawn to a powerful presence within himself. It was him, but not him. Lan knew this was Gavilan. He saw himself in a strange place, with four people beside him. One had wings that radiated light at the tips. His connection to her was so deep, it took his breath away. The others connected to him in a different way and seemed to be on a mission of some sort. There was a small, but intense-looking girl, a lanky red-headed boy, and one who could have been a boy or a girl. Together, they focused on a brooding city in front of them. It seemed to suck all light out of the air. Each of them held a crystal of a different shape in their hand. Lan felt both excitement and fear for what was about to happen.

Lan's vision faded away and he felt the presence of Boosha through the Golden Grid. She whispered, "May you become a Crystalline Expression of the Balance of All That Is." The butterfly lifted off his body and flew into the air to join the cloud of others that fluttered overhead. Once again, he noticed the sun had shifted position and was now straight overhead. It seemed to Lan like only moments had passed since he first watched the blue butterfly flutter toward him. Instead, hours had gone by.

Still half in and half out of his vision, he reached for his Map Compass to anchor himself. Just before turning it over and seeing the needle make the sweep that indicated the device was working, Lan heard the whisper, "That was The Mastery, the Third Key."

Lan felt disoriented getting up and continuing his journey. Everything looked the same as before, but he felt so different inside. He was himself and yet not himself. At the very least he must have grown a foot, he felt so tall. Filled with joy, he imagined himself with Boosha now. He'd tower over her!

Not even his usual doubts about what he was going to do with the Three Keys kept him from feeling the giddy joy of the moment. He kept smiling and then laughing for no reason. The trees shimmered even more vibrantly than before and he could actually see the Golden Grid for a while. Moving swiftly, he covered a lot of territory in his new state of freedom.

Laughing at the antics of a squirrel above him, he came around a bend and stopped. In front of him stood a wasteland without a single tree, bush, or plant on it. The soil was hard, white and cracked. On the other side, the forest glimmered tantalizingly but nothing bridged the two sides.

Everything in Lan recoiled at the thought of crossing this barren spot. The soil was so baked the air didn't even pick up dust from the surface. He squinted at some forms in the middle. What was out there?

Wanting to get a bigger view of it all, Lan climbed a tree behind him. After the ravine, he'd learned the value of taking a moment to figure out his next move. Maybe he could skirt around the wasteland, or maybe he'd find a special path through it. But as far as he could see, that dead swath of land cut the forest in two. He couldn't even locate the Golden Grid in this part of the forest.

A flash of red lifted off some shapes in the center, catching his eye. How odd, Lan thought. What was that? He peered at the forms, then shuddered as he realized what they were. Skeletons in red clothes. Once again, The Gatherers had been taken care of as the Mother Tree had promised. But if they couldn't get across the Badlands, how could he? After climbing down, Lan consulted the Map Compass. With a sigh, he discovered it had stopped moving again. It had been working before he reached the Badlands, so there must be some reason he was supposed to stop here, besides the obvious one that he couldn't cross the wasteland without risking his life.

He saw a picture in his mind of the Mother Tree. "Heal the land," she whispered to him.

At that request, Lan stalled for time. How could he do that? "What happened here?" Lan asked her from his mind.

"In the time before The Shift, there were bad substances that humans used for producing energy. When they were done with them, they buried the substances here. They killed all life." As always when she talked, Lan saw picture-feelings. He watched as men in white suits dug holes and buried boxes with skulls painted on them. Whatever they had buried began to leak out of the containers and into the soil. Slowly all life withered and died. The Mother Tree showed him how she and the other trees had managed to contain the poison by strengthening their roots at the edge of the wasteland but they could not heal the damaged land.

"We need your help. Use the Three Keys."

Lan flushed red. There it was again! That assumption from others that he knew what to do with the Three Keys. He hadn't figured out how he was going to deliver the Three Keys when he arrived in Asira yet, and here he was being told to heal something, for heaven's sake. Agitated, he strode up the edge of the Badlands. He was going to fail at this and everything else he was supposed to do. He screamed inside, "I can't do this. Don't ask me!" The Mother Tree soothed him, reassured him. As if he were one of her seedlings, she filled him with green nectar. Lan felt his doubt shift into confidence.

Looking up, he saw greenish light shimmering in the air over the trees. Suddenly Lan felt compelled to take out the crystal. Striding back to his pack, he pulled it out. As he turned it over in his hands, the iridescent colors shot out, mixing with the green light. And just like that, he knew what to do. Or at least he knew how to start.

Reaching into his bag, he took out the wooden staves that he and Sawyer had carved. Holding the crystal in one hand and the staves in the other, Lan spoke the Invocation to the Four Directions. As he finished with the last direction, he set Empowerment on the dirt where nothing grew. He repeated the same words that Boosha had said to him. "May you honor the innate wisdom within all life."

A loud crack! and the land began to move, heaving up and down the gap. It reminded Lan of someone who had drowned and then come back to life as it gasped and gulped. By the time the ground stopped moving, there was a new color on the land about a third of the way across. The soil had changed from white to a reddish brown.

Lan tentatively stepped out onto the soil. He knew he had to go up to the edge where the new soil met the sick soil, but he was nervous that he would end up like one of The Gatherers. He felt a gentle push on his back from the tree behind him. Grabbing his pack, crystal and staves, he set off to the new edge.

Setting Empowerment down on the next band of white, cracked soil, Lan said, "May you remember, honor, and protect your gifts."

Once again came the loud cracking sounds as the land in front of Lan began to heave and move. This time it reminded him of when the village cow began giving birth. Her sides had heaved and shifted as the calf made its way out into the world. Part of Lan's mind watched the unfolding, but part of him thought it was odd to speak those words to soil. He wasn't sure he entirely understood them for himself, much less this.

The sun was low in the sky when the land stopped moving. Lan could see there was still a section of the Badlands that needed restoring. This time he moved quickly to the new edge. Placing Empowerment down on the last dead strip, he said the words of the Third Key that he'd only heard himself for the first time that morning. "May you become a Crystalline Expression of The Balance of All That Is."

This time the land made a noise that sounded like the wailing of a person crouched over a loved one in the last moments of life. The trees on both sides began to move, weeping with the land. A great cloud of sadness lifted out of the soil and drifted into the sky.

All around Lan, from one edge of the forest to the other, lay healthy, life-supporting soil. He was awed at the sight of it. He still had no idea how to deliver the Three Keys or even to who in Asira, but he knew beyond a doubt how powerful they were.

Lan sent a silent question to the Mother Tree. "Is it done?"

"Almost," she replied. Then she showed him what to do next. Moving back to the middle of the former Badlands, Lan took the staves and began setting them out in circles around him, singing their names as he did, "Birch, Hawthorn, Ash, may you grow here. Alder, Oak, Willow, may you grow here. Apple, Spruce, Cherry, may you grow here. Aspen, Maple, Cypress, may you grow here, too." Then he gave a resounding finish to his song, "Aaaannnnnddddd Pecan!"

Taking out his cloak, Lan lay down in the middle of his tree circles and watched the Double Moons rise. A tiredness like he'd never felt before swept over him and his eyes dropped as if wearing weights.

That night he dreamed he'd become a tree again, like he had with the birches. He felt his roots sink into the ground, connecting with all the other roots. Those roots then connected to the Golden Grid. His trunk sent out wild, alive cries of celebration and his branches embraced himself as Gavilan. Looking out, the whole Forest was celebrating the return of the trees to the wasteland. Lan stretched and smiled in his sleep.

CHAPTER TEN

ARRIVING

Lan opened his eyes and tried to sit up. Something held him down. Lifting his head, he stared in astonishment at the sight around him. The entire area of scorched dirt between the two forests vibrated in lush green. Little seedlings of different trees, as well as a vine with purple flowers, had sprouted during the night. He was covered in it. After pulling it off his body, Lan sat in wonderment at the change all around him.

The trees on both sides quivered, flashing their leaves from dark to light in the sunlight. Lan wondered if they were expressing excitement or joy or something else. The Mother Tree flashed in his mind and said, "Yes! They are connected again." Lan sunk his hands into the rich, loamy dirt and felt the roots and fungi crisscrossing in their net of partnership. What had been a barren wasteland just a couple of days ago had been transformed into a fertile, life supporting area again. Lan felt a wave of appreciation surge toward him from the trees as their boughs moved in what looked like applause. He ducked his head in embarrassment, then stood up and took an elaborate bow to mock his hero status. He should put on the cloak and really get a standing ovation!

Lan shook the leaves out of his hair and clothes and prepared to take up his journey. He instinctively knew the Map Compass was working again, but he glanced at it just to make sure. Picking up his bow, quiver and pack, he strode to the edge of the forest. He took one last look at the amazing change of the Badlands. He'd have to start calling them the Good Lands now, and smiled at the thought. Adjusting the energy in his Dantians along with his bow, Lan turned toward Asira and took off at a lope. He was getting close now.

As Lan easily covered mile after mile each day, he noticed how differently he felt. Thinking back on his first few days in the Forest, he marveled at the changes. The wisdom he'd gained from the Mother Tree, and the birch dance had shifted his sense of belonging in the world. His time with Sawyer had given him answers about his past. But it was getting his third initiation and then using the Three Keys that seemed to have changed him the most. Lan didn't know if it was his imagination, but his eyesight seemed to have improved. And not by a little but by a lot. He could see the details of a leaf on a tree across a clearing in stunning clarity and every blade of grass shimmered and stood out from its neighbor

Around the time he noticed his vision improving, the hawk showed up again. Lan didn't know if it was the exact same one from the black ravine, but he liked to think it was. The raptor was so silent, Lan only noticed it when its shadow passed over him. By the time he looked up, it was usually disappearing behind a tree. Occasionally, he'd see the hawk on a branch, watching him. Lan's heart always lifted at the sight of it. Maybe it was just his imagination but the hawk seemed like a guardian angel, or maybe a messenger from Boosha.

As days passed, Lan's new sense of himself began to feel normal and self-doubt began to creep back. His thoughts tumbled around in his head, searching for answers he didn't have. He still wasn't sure how he was going to deliver the Three Keys in Asira when he arrived. They were inside of him! Then he wondered why they needed them. Would his next task be like saving the Badlands, or something else? What if he couldn't help this town called Asira?

A new thought crept around the edges of Lan's mind. Boosha had told him to give the crystal cube called Empowerment to this village. But he didn't want to. He liked how he felt when he played with it, watching the swirling colors in the center. It soothed his anxiety and left him peaceful and calm. After the healing of the Badlands, he'd grown even more attached to it. Boosha had told him to keep the name secret. Did he tell the name to the villagers when he gave it to them?

After spending half a day worrying about what he would do when he got to Asira, Lan then spent half a day worrying about what he would do after he completed his mission. If he didn't stay too long, he'd have time to return through the forest before the coldest part of winter caught up to him again. He imagined his joyful return to his home village. Sometimes he played out a returning hero scene where everyone through a big party for him. Other times he just saw

Boosha's happy and proud face. Then his mind got practical and he wondered if the Map Compass would show him the way back. If it didn't, he wasn't sure what he would do. The Forest of Dandaka was immense. Would he be able to find his way back without the Map Compass? Maybe the trees themselves would show him.

The morning arrived when he looked at the Map Compass and realized he could reach Asira that day. How odd to think he was almost done with this journey. He wished he could do something about his appearance as his traveling clothes had become rough-looking and probably quite smelly. His hair had grown tremendously long and by the feel of it, had snarled in knots. His mind had focused so intently in the past months on simply making it to Asira, he'd never spent any time on grooming. He stopped at a stream and washed up the best he could. Taking out his knife, he cut through the worst of the hair snarls and combed his fingers through what was left. Lan imagined he must look like a shaggy, unkempt dog.

Briefly contemplating putting the cloak on over his travel-worn clothes, Lan shook his head. It still felt too fancy for him. He didn't want to put people off with an exaggerated or grand appearance, but just show up as one of them. In his mind, Lan imagined the village to be like the home he'd left behind.

And just like that, Lan walked out of the forest and found himself looking at the village. He could see people walking around. No one noticed him. "Hey!" he yelled, waving his arms. Nothing changed. Maybe that was for the best for the moment. How strange, Lan told himself, to be in the presence of humans again.

Lan started muttering under his breath, "Hello, citizens of Asira. I am Lan and I have brought you the Three Keys and the crystal Empowerment. Here you go!" He could imagine the looks he'd get with that opening line. He tried again. "Hello! I am Lan and I've just travelled through the Forest of Dandaka. I've brought you a message from my village." That one felt awkward, too. He wondered if these people had the same dread of the forest as the people of his village did.

So intent was Lan on what he was going to say, it took a moment for him to realize a river separated the forest from the village. And not just any river. It was wide and by the look of the water, extremely deep. Lan knew that the calmer and darker the water, the more powerful the current. Throwing a stick into the water, he gloomily watched as the river grabbed it and took it away from his vision in just seconds.

All right, Lan thought, there has to be a bridge somewhere. Wondering if it was above or below him, he looked at the Map Compass. Classic! It had gone silent again and didn't even give an indication of a large river. He decided to start searching upstream. A little extra time getting across would give him a chance to figure out the perfect thing to say, anyway.

Lan was soon above the village. He knew bridges were built in narrower spots, but the river showed no signs of changing size. Every now and then, he climbed a tree and scanned for a bridge or some other way across, but saw nothing. A little after noon, he reversed direction and ran downstream. After the town, the ground began dropping off more steeply. The water moved even more rapidly than before.

Late in the day, Lan felt and heard a deep roar ahead. The sound rumbled through his bones. Coming around a bend, he stopped short on the edge of a cliff. The river neither cared nor resisted the threshold in the full power of its flow. Sucking in his breath, Lan stood mesmerized at the sight, watching the water at the point of its change in course. Some of it became mist, while some of it separated into individual droplets that hung in the air, filled with light, for a moment. The rest fell in twisted braids of water. Almost black above the falls, the water, free from the riverbanks, turned a glorious green and white.

After a while, Lan shook himself out of his fascination. Turning, he headed back upriver. He still hadn't figured out how to get across. His backup plan had been to float across on a log but after seeing the waterfall, he feared he'd get sucked down the river faster than he could make his way across.

By the time he reached his starting point across from the village, the sun had set. The light would disappear quickly now, so Lan made camp. He hesitated to make a fire. Would it draw unwanted attention to himself? He decided to play it safe while he continued to figure out the situation, and drew back into the forest. He immediately felt safer in the company of his brother and sister trees.

That night Lan had a strange dream. He became the hawk watching a boy walk toward a pile of boulders and bushes. Through his hawk eyes, he watched as the boy bent down under a bush and then completely disappeared. Giving a cry, he rose in the air and flew across the water toward the village. Next he saw the boy emerging on the other side of the river.

In the morning Lan awoke slowly, remembering the feeling of flying. He had decided he would walk back upriver far enough away from the village and the waterfall that he could float across on a log. Hopefully he could make it across before he was swept too far downriver. His plan was to locate the narrowest part of the river, find a flat log to hang onto and carry his pack and bow without getting them wet, and just kick like crazy to get across.

As Lan walked back upriver, he found himself eyeing piles of brush and rocks. He gave one a closer look and discovered it really was just a pile of rocks with some bushes growing nearby. Then, in front of him, he saw the exact spot that he'd dreamed about. The whole thing stood in crystal clarity, shimmering in the daylight.

Approaching slowly, Lan wasn't sure if he hoped to find out his dream was real or just a dream. Pushing a branch to the side, he saw the opening in the rocks and knew it had all been real. His heart pounded and his throat squeezed closed at the thought of entering the opening. Still, in his dream he had made it to the other side so that gave him some courage, even if it felt like he was faking it. He'd never been a fan of tight places.

After deciding to use the tunnel, Lan's mind went into strategy mode. How was he going to see in there? Deciding to experiment, Lan grabbed his fire kit and a stick and lit the end. Then he crawled a little way into the passage. As soon as he moved, the flame on the stick went out and just became a smoldering ember. Blackness wrapped itself around Lan. Backing up, he retreated to the entrance, wondering how to make a better torch.

His mind flashed back to Sawyer. They had been working over a fire in front of the house before it was destroyed by the Mammophants. Sawyer was showing Lan how to make pitch sticks out of pine sap. It was a tricky process as the sap melted over a fire. Too hot and it could quickly ignite. As the mixture fully melted, Sawyer showed Lan how to add crushed charcoal and then cattail fluff. Finally, they dipped the tips of short sticks into the black, gooey mixture and shaped them into long ovals. Sawyer then showed Lan how to reheat the pitch stick and use it as glue, to patch a hole in a container, or even to light a fire if all the wood was wet.

Lan pulled his pine pitch sticks out of his pack. He had six. Not sure if they would work as a torch or how long they would burn if they did, he also had to figure out how to handle them inside a dark space. He'd need to have the remainder close at hand, if the first started burning low. Trying to light one in the dark with his flint would be impossible.

Tucking the spare pine sticks in his pocket, Lan pulled out his fire kit. He'd start a very small tinder bundle with his char cloth and then light the first pitch stick. Once his mini torch was lit he'd have to move quickly through the tunnel. Gathering his packs and slinging his bow over his shoulder, he lit his improvised torch, then sprang eagerly into the passageway. Now that he'd made his decision, he wasn't going to hesitate.

The packed earth floor descended quickly. For a brief moment, Lan wondered who had made this tunnel and if it was used by anyone today. The air grew colder and damper the further he descended. At first the walls were made of dirt with tree roots running through them. Lan loved touching the root grids that the Mother Tree had shown him. When he did, though, he got the sense that something alive was trapped in the dirt. Lan sent a question into the roots, not knowing if he would get an answer or not. "Who are you?"

"I am Empowerment, the Earth Spirit," Lan heard. The voice sounded strained, as if it were being squeezed. In his mind rose an image of an immense being with wings made of trees and a body covered by plants. Its claws were root-like and it had teeth of glittering crystals. Lan was startled that the voice called itself Empowerment. He barely began to form a question about the crystal cube that he carried when the Earth Spirit responded.

"Yes, you carry my spirit with you. You have used it already to heal the earth in the Badlands. Because of your service you were shown this labyrinth to cross the river."

Labyrinth! Lan had never heard that word before. Before he could ponder its meaning, he came to a fork in the tunnel. One path turned sharply to his left while the other continued straight. The walls were damper, oozing mud. He hesitated, trying to determine which way to go. Deciding to go straight, he took two steps in that direction and almost lost his light as the pitch torch dimmed. Lan backed up, grabbing another pine pitch stick.

Stopping to light the new torch, Lan glanced down and spied a folded piece of paper. Picking up the damp parchment, Lan discovered a drawing showing him the way through the maze. It contained various colors and a legend explaining the different sections. He read Water Spirit, Earth Spirit, Fire Spirit and Air Spirit, and then words that made his knees quiver. The legend said, "Evil Spirit." What could that possibly be?

Mindful of the short amount of time that the torch would provide light, Lan turned to his left. His mouth dropped open in wonder. He found himself surrounded by a wall of water, creating a tunnel. He couldn't resist placing his hand on it, and discovered the water to be hard and unyielding. But then he tried sticking his finger into the wall of water, and the liquid gave way, allowing his finger to pass right through. How strange, Lan thought, it's both hard and soft! Retracting his finger, the water wall immediately closed up around the hole he'd made. Although it swirled in waves, he could see fish and water plants on the other side. Again he had a sense of something alive trapped in the sides of the tunnel.

Before he could even open his mouth to speak, Lan heard, "I am Water Spirit."

Always ready to ask a weird question Lan responded with, "Do you have a name, too?"

"Only to those who can command the Water Spirit."

Lan wondered who would dare command such a powerful being. Was this tunnel an example of what they commanded it to do? He wished he'd thought to ask the Earth Spirit that same question. At a loss of what one said to a Water Spirit, he asked for advice. "Do you have any wisdom for me?"

He heard a watery chuckle, then wild laughter, reminding Lan of someone choking on a liquid. "Yes. Beware of the Fire Spirit."

Turning a corner, Lan entered a particularly black section of the passageway. His second torch was burning low so he took out his third pine pitch stick. Touching it to the still-burning torch, he heard a crack and a loud whoosh of flame. The walls and ceiling caught on fire. This wasn't just any fire, though, but alive and leaping in its power. Most of all, it seemed angry.

"You would be mad, too," spoke the Fire Spirit. "I have been trapped here long before The Shift. I need air to burn and right now the only air is within you."

Lan heard a command of "Move it!" from the Earth Spirit. As he sprinted forward, he felt the air in his lungs being sucked out. He could barely stand. Dropping to his knees, he began crawling. He found it cooler down by the dirt floor, with more air to breathe. But even that began to disappear and Lan's vision darkened. Just when he thought he was going to pass out completely and be consumed by the fire, he turned another corner.

The cool, damp air of the Earth Spirit surrounded him again. Leaning against the wall, Lan stopped to recover his breath and calm himself. Too late he remembered how to protect his Middle Dantian, the energy center of his heart and breath. If he ran into the needy Fire Spirit again he'd use some of the techniques Sawyer had shown him. He smelled something that reminded him of a wet dog and he tentatively put his hand up to his hair. It was completely singed. Panicking, he reached further back and checked his bow. It seemed to be okay.

As Lan regained control of his breath, he felt a wave of tiredness descend over him. Was that his imagination or was he being slowly pulled into the oozing wall? "Earth Spirit," Lan asked, "What's going on? Are you there?"

Silence was the response. Lan felt an awareness in the black goo, but it did not communicate with him. The more Lan tried to talk with it, the stronger it pulled him in. In his mind, Lan saw visions of animals and plants pulled into the substance and slowly turned into black goo. Lan's nose filled with the fetid smell of decay and the stench of ancient death. Thrashing and struggling, Lan felt himself gripped even tighter. And still he was being slowly sucked in. The goo had reached his face and covered half his torso. Only the lower parts of his arms and legs were free. Much more of this and he would suffocate.

Lan stopped to catch his breath and calm his thoughts. What would Sawyer tell him to do right now? He began chanting his true name under his breath, "Gavilan, Gavilan, Gavilan." Then he activated his three Dantians and began running energy in the Cosmic Orbit. His inner strength returned and Lan slowly began to extricate himself as if he were swimming in slow motion. With one last slow-motion movement, Lan freed himself, collapsing onto the floor of the tunnel.

Miraculously, Lan's torch was still burning, but he could tell it only held a few moments of light. He quickly took out another torch and lit it, then looked at the labyrinth map and moved forward on his hands and knees. Still crawling through the tunnel of black goo, Lan kept his mind focused by continuing to chant his name. Rounding a corner, Lan, felt a bit of air stir the heavy smell of the tunnel. Maybe he was almost through this labyrinth! But when he studied the paper map, Lan saw he only made it halfway.

Suddenly, he was enveloped in a roaring wind that blew dirt in his eyes and buffeted him on all sides. He felt the parchment ripped out of his hands and then his torch flickered out. Just as suddenly, he was out of the wind. Lan was too panicked in the dark to communicate with the Air Spirit. His sense of adventure had blown away with the wind and he just wanted this long nightmare to end. What if he took a wrong turn and got lost in the labyrinth forever? He remembered the hawk dream and watching the boy come out the other side to quiet his fear.

Crawling forward, Lan bumped into the wall of the tunnel. He tentatively reached out to touch it and was relieved when he discovered dirt. Lan immediately connected with Earth Spirit and asked for help and guidance. His eyes shifted and he began to "see" as the roots did to navigate in the dirt. He could make out the dim shape of the tunnel to his right so he turned that way. He knew he could stand upright and walk if he wanted to, but somehow staying close to the ground seemed safer to him.

Turning another corner, everything went dark again. He felt the oozing awareness of the Evil Spirit on his right and shuddered. Then

Lan felt the coolness of the Water Spirit on his left so he focused on that. Talking with the Water Spirit was a bit like conversing with a wild child who just wanted to play. Nothing the Water Spirit said made any sense. Lan wasn't sure what he'd do if he had to make a choice of direction, but for now he was still moving forward.

Lan's head bumped into a wall of black goo that immediately began sucking him in again. Slowly backing up, Lan stopped. He was at a dead end. On his left was the Water Spirit and on his right was the Evil Spirit. Had he missed a turn? Should he attempt to go back? A wild idea sprouted in his mind. What if he could wade through the Water Spirit wall and get to the other side? Part of his mind retreated from the thought. Maybe floating across the river and chancing the waterfall would be easier but, oh, going back would be a nightmare.

Calling on Hawk to guide him, Lan launched himself into the Water Spirit wall. It promptly bounced him back with a wet slap. Remembering how he'd been able to penetrate the wall with his finger, Lan stretched out his fingertips and lightly touched the water. They slipped in easily. He wondered if there was a better place of entry and tried the same thing in a different place. By trial-and-error, he discovered it was easiest to insert his fingers into the wall when he was close to the floor. Lan gulped a lungful of air, held his breath, and made another try at easing into the water wall.

This time, it worked! Lan could see a bit better in the water, but found it difficult to move. He couldn't swim with his arms and legs and felt trapped under the weight of the water. Was this the end? He'd heard that if someone was about to die, all the events of their life would pass through their mind but none of that was happening. A fish swept passed him on the right and Lan inched slightly over to follow. He entered a current and shot forward like a rocket. Lan's body was propelled up the side, across the top, down the side and then across the bottom twice in a dizzying spin. In desperation, he sent his upper Dantian energy out like a finger as he approached the side again. The energy created an opening and he spilled out. The Water Spirit closed the wall behind him.

Lan crawled forward by the slight glow of the water tunnel behind him. Turning a corner, everything went pitch black again. He knew he was back in the evil black goo again. Lan began feeling the sides of the tunnel around him without letting it suck him in. There was an opening to his left and also one straight ahead. Which way should he go? Before he panicked completely, Lan heard panting coming toward him. What could that be? Suddenly, Lan felt his cheek licked by a tongue and heard happy growling. Reaching up, he felt a wiggly, hairy body. A dog! He wasn't alone anymore and this dog must know the way out. His relief was so immense he threw his arms around his unseen rescuer in gratitude.

Lan thought he'd first heard the panting coming from his left so he started to move in that direction. He hoped the dog would stay by his side but the animal blocked him from moving forward. He tried to move around the dog to continue down the passageway, but again the friendly creature stood firmly in his way. Finally, Lan moved in the other direction and the dog turned and walked beside him. Gradually it grew lighter and Lan could see his companion that had saved him. He was bigger than any dog he'd seen in his village with a head twice the size of most dogs' heads. Its hair was more like fur. Lan knew exactly how soft it was, too.

He took a moment to bury his face in that soft fur and hug the dog or whatever it was in gratitude and then stood up. He was back in the Earth Spirit tunnel and, after his knees stopped shaking, he sprinted for the exit. When Lan burst out into the open from behind some rocks he saw he was on the other side of the river. The Hawk vision had been right. He'd made it through the tunnel, but a few details had sure been left out of that vision.

Lan felt strange as he looked around and found himself on this side of the river and the Forest on the far side. He felt exposed without the trees. His dog savior was nowhere in sight. Looking up toward the village, he saw a group of people gathered on top of the incline, pointing down at him. He raised his arm in greeting and began striding up the hill. He'd finally arrived at Asira!

CHAPTER ELEVEN

PAINFUL LESSONS

Asira finished packing. The only chore left was to take down her simple hut and return everything else to her parent's home.

Susie burst into her small home, making it instantly crowded. "Come quick!" she said, tugging on Asira's arm.

"Why?" Asira snapped back, irritated with the interruption. "I'm getting ready to move back home."

"You are?" Susie looked around in surprise, but she was too distracted with her other news to take in this sudden change in Asira's plans.

"Yes," Asira answered curtly, then handed her a pile of bedding. "As long as you're here, you can help me."

As short as Asira was, Susie still had to trot to keep up with her as they headed back to the village. Her voice was muffled behind the big stack of blankets. "Asira, someone has arrived in the village."

Asira stopped. Maybe she shouldn't risk going to the village at all. "Is it one of the visitors?" she asked.

"I don't think so," Susie replied, still trying to talk and hang on to her load. "People are saying there's something different about him.

He says he's brought something for us."

Asira flashed back to the lone figure she'd seen from the bluff. "Was he wearing a blue cloak or coat?"

"I don't know," Susie responded. "I haven't seen him myself. They put him in the visitor's hut while they're waiting for Kuut to come back." The Director was gone on a trip. No one was sure where he had gone or when he'd get back.

Asira made a dismissive gesture with her hand. "This has nothing to do with me. Let's get going." Turning back to the path, she took off again.

"He keeps asking, 'Is this Asira?'" Susie said.

Asira felt her breathing stop for a moment at the mention of her name.

"It's weird, he's not asking for you," Susie continued "It's like he thinks Asira is the name of a place or something."

Asira's heart lifted for a moment, then her features scowled. This was messing up her plans. People were going to start looking for her. If she left at this moment, they'd think she'd run away and her carefully created story would be worthless. Then her parents would be in danger of Kuut's retaliation.

Reaching her parents' home, Asira ducked in quickly with Susie close behind her. Grabbing both her parents' hands, she pulled them into a corner and tried to speak calmly but her eyes moved wildly like those of a trapped animal. "You know about this visitor? What should I do?" she whispered to them.

"I think you should just slip away," Ryan told her. "We'll tell them your story and that you left a couple of days before this new visitor even showed up." Asira nodded, gulping back her tears now that it was the moment to say goodbye. Her mom hugged her and whispered a gentle blessing to her, "May you stay safe and find all that your heart desires."

Asira glanced over at Susie, who stayed on the other side of the room pretending the agitated whispering was none of her business. Seeing past her act of nonchalance, Asira pulled away from her parents and came over to her. Bending down, she hugged her and whispered, "I have to go away for a while to get more herbs. If anyone asks, tell them I'll be back soon. Be a good helper to mom and dad and don't be sad while I'm gone."

Susie slowly nodded her head, her eyes prickling with tears. First Takaani and now Asira was leaving. Would she really come back? Susie brushed her eyes with the back of her hand, then put on her bravest smile for her beloved sister. "You'll come back with lots of great stories, right?"

"That's my sis!" Asira acknowledged the silent pact between them. Then she silently slipped out, returning to her hut to finish packing and prepare for the unknown road ahead of her. A shadow crossed the opening. Startled, she looked up, then was knocked down as Takaani jumped on her and began excitedly licking her face.

"Takaani!" Asira exclaimed, getting to her knees. "What are you doing here?" His only answer was to wave his tail with even more happiness. She halted her packing for a moment to savor being with him again. Wrapping her arms around him, she touched her forehead to his. Her breath synchronized with his steady inhale and exhale and then she felt their heartbeats connect in tempo. A wave of peace swept over her as all her doubts disappeared.

"Okay," Asira said. "Let's go." Shouldering her pack, Asira took one last look at her little home, sending her appreciation into the rock wall and the earthen floor for sheltering her. With one hand on Takaani's head, she stepped out and began walking toward the mountain.

Lan stared at the mirror. He had never seen one before. It reminded him of a frozen lake hanging on the wall. He couldn't figure out how it worked, but he was even more bemused and startled by his appearance in it. Was that really him standing there? He couldn't believe how much he'd changed since leaving Boosha. His hair had grown long and hung below his shoulders. He knew he was taller, but he was also leaner from days of running. But the most startling change of all was his eyes. They were brilliant, clear and golden. The times he'd seen his reflection before his eyes had always looked brown. Lan couldn't figure out if it was the difference between seeing his reflection in a mirror instead of water or if his eyes had changed color somehow. Briefly he remembered the third activation, then shook his head. That couldn't explain the change in his eyes.

Lan puzzled over what to do next. Just like his appearance, this arrival in Asira wasn't anything like he'd imagined. The first people of the village who met him when he'd emerged from the tunnel two days ago acted strange. On the surface they were friendly to him, but they seemed scared, too. After the initial greetings, they asked him where'd he'd come from. When he said the Forest of Dandaka, they all pulled back a bit. The younger children kept staring at his face. He thought he must be covered in mud and grime, but now as he looked at himself in the mirror he wondered if it was because of the odd color of his eyes.

Lan asked them if this was "Asira" but he just got more strange looks with that question and no one answered him. Then they asked him if he was here to buy something from them. "No," Lan replied. "I've been sent here to give you something." That stopped all conversation.

Someone led him to a special building reserved for the visitors who arrived seasonally. There he had the opportunity to bathe and found fresh clothes, soft and beautifully embroidered, laid out for him. Lan felt a little ridiculous at first when he put them on, but he was very grateful for the new pair of shoes that came with the outfit. When he saw himself in the mirror, looking so entirely different from before, he stopped worrying about the fancy clothes. They seemed to fit him well. Even though the end of his journey wasn't turning out like he'd expected, he took it as a good sign that these villagers were treating him well. They served him meals several times a day and everyone was polite, if distant. If he tried to start a conversation and ask what was going on, people would just nod, smile and leave.

With so much spare time suddenly on his hands, Lan didn't quite know what to do with himself. He took everything out of his pack and repacked it. He wished he had his Tree Staves to consult to get some answers.

Lan figured out quickly that if he stayed in the village, he was free to go wherever he wanted, but if he attempted to leave, someone suddenly appeared to silently blocking his way. Was he a prisoner or was something else going on?

The first couple of days, he'd enjoyed seeing all the differences in this town versus his own village. The houses here were built from whitewashed stone in a round design. The roofs featured beams coming to a point and covered with straw thatching. The buildings had plenty of windows and felt airy and light inside. Back in his home village, the square, wooden houses seemed small and dark in comparison. The homes he saw now were definitely more elegant. Lan was intrigued by the windows, which contained smaller pieces of hard, clear rock like the mirror, but without a reflection. It seemed to Lan that his village tried to not call any attention to itself, while this town seemed to strut its wealth and wanted to stand out.

Today Lan walked through the market. Many of the products being sold he'd never seen before and he wondered what they were. He saw several of the mirror objects, and a lot of metal items they didn't have back home. He wondered if he could barter for some to take back to his friends, Sam and John. Lan picked up a container made out of another clear, hard substance. He was about to ask what it was and how it was used, when out of the corner of his eye, he noticed a small girl watching him. She seemed friendly and looked like she wanted to interact with him. Acting as if he hadn't noticed her, Lan returned to his temporary home. The girl burst in behind him.

"Hi! I'm Susie," she said. In spite of being slightly out of breath, she appeared pleased with her boldness.

Lan replied with a short greeting. He wasn't sure if this small person could help him figure out what was going on, or if she was just going to be a nuisance.

"Why are you here?" she asked.

Lan's tense shoulders dropped and he smiled. Finally! Maybe he was about to get some answers.

Lan repeated what he'd said already to others. "If this is Asira, then I have things to deliver."

Susie cocked her head, as if sizing him up. Lan wondered if she thought he was dim-witted because she spoke very slowly. "This is Our Place. Asira is my sister."

Lan flushed with sudden awareness. Oh my Earth, he thought, I'm so stupid. No wonder everyone's been treating me like the village idiot.

He opened his mouth to ask her more questions, when he became aware of a commotion outside. A group of people were coming toward his house. Susie ducked behind a free standing closet and whispered, "Don't tell them I'm here. Kuut must be back."

Lan's mind tried to take it all in. "Who's Kuut?" he managed to ask, but Susie didn't have a chance to answer before several people burst into his cottage.

"Come with us," a tall, burly man spoke curtly.

As usual, no one answered him when he asked "Why?"

Lan followed the small group, glancing over his shoulder in time to see Susie slip out of the building and trail behind. She reminded him of himself back in the village with Boosha, able to disappear in a crowd of people.

The burly man led Lan into the largest circular building in the village, Lan felt nervous. Everyone seemed to be there, sitting several deep around the edge. The center was empty. At one end stood a large, ornate chair. At first, Lan thought the seat was for him but no one asked him to sit down. He stood awkwardly in the middle. With everyone's eyes on him, Lan cringed inwardly. This was what he'd spent his whole life avoiding. It would have been easier to have his teeth pulled out then stared at in this way. He caught sight of Susie behind everyone, close to the door and felt slightly better.

The heavy silence was deafening. Lan figured they must be waiting for this Kuut guy Susie had mentioned. He tried to focus on his Dantians and his breathing but his nerves continued to get the better of him. His body jerked uncontrollably and he hoped no one noticed. He forced himself to remain still, but of course everyone had noticed. There was nothing else to watch.

A large, bearded man dressed in richly embroidered clothes, with a long cape, strode in. His dark brown hair was swept back from his face and glistened with something that held it in place. It was obvious this man highly admired his own beard because it was elaborately combed, braided and even had a few pieces of jewelry woven in it. Lan turned, along with everyone else, to face him.

"Greetings!" the man boomed. Coming up behind Lan, he held out his hand, then grasped Lan's upper arm as they shook hands. The man's face was all smiles but his dark brown eyes were hard as flinty rocks as they took in Lan's appearance. Lan's skin crawled at the man's touch and he fought the urge to pull back. He smiled nervously.

"I am Kuut, Director of Our Place. I'm sorry I wasn't here to greet you when you arrived." Kuut strode over to the elaborately decorated chair and sat down. "Now let's hear all about you!"

Lan shifted from foot to foot. And hesitated. He wasn't sure which energy to respond to, the open and welcoming one or the hard, impenetrable one. He opened his mouth and to his horror, found himself stuttering. "I...I...I..."

Kuut stopped him by forcefully raising his hand. A look of irritation flashed across his face, but his words were jovial. "Come now. No need to play the shy maiden with me! What is your name and where are you from?"

"I am Lan and I come from the other side of the Forest of Dandaka," he finally managed to croak. He wished he had some water, for his mouth was parched. He looked around to see if anyone would offer him something to drink, but no one was offering anything but more silence. His statement was received, though, with wide eyes and dropped mouths.

Kuut stroked his beard as he contemplated Lan. "You came

through the forest? No one travels in the Forest of Dandaka. How long did it take you? What was it like?"

Lan hedged the truth slightly. "It took me seven months." He didn't mention three of those months had been spent with Sawyer. "It was hard." Lan felt protective of the forest. He didn't want others to go there.

"Well," Kuut said, "I bet you have some great adventures to share with us tonight over dinner. So tell me, how can we be of service to you? I hear you've been asking for our Asira."

Lan felt disoriented. Every fiber of his being was screaming not to trust this man, yet he'd only just found out that Asira wasn't a village but a person. Should he keep silent about what Boosha had told him to do?

Lan hedged the truth. "I was asked by my grandmother to bring something to Asira."

"You'll have to tell me more about this grandmother of yours tonight at dinner," Kuut said. "She sounds interesting." Reaching behind him, Kuut lifted something out of a pack. Lan's body involuntarily twitched when he realized his pack with all of his possessions was sitting behind Kuut's chair.

"Is this what you were bringing Asira?" He held up the crystal. Empowerment sat flat and lifeless in Kuut's hand, no flashing colors. Lan felt himself grow cold, then desperate, when Kuut held up the Map Compass. "Or was it this?"

Mutely, he pointed to the crystal. He hoped he was just being over reactive and these people could be trusted, but he felt like he was standing in front of the hawthorn tree again.

"Are you here to get a healing from Asira, then?" Still unable to speak, Lan nodded his head. He had no idea what Kuut was talking about. Why hadn't Boosha explained better what he was supposed to do? "What's wrong with you? You look healthy enough." The words flew out of Kuut and pinned him to an invisible target where all he could do was squirm.

Lan split into two parts. One part was frozen, watching as a different Lan spoke. "I get bad headaches and I can't see like I used to."

Kuut picked up Lan's bow. "Well, I can see that would be a problem for a hunter like you." Frozen, Lan watched in horror as Kuut stroked the limb of his bow, then casually plucked the string as if it were a musical instrument. Lan slowed his breath to stop himself from screaming, "Stop touching my bow!"

Kuut ducked his head as if thinking. Then he looked straight into Lan's eyes and said, "Well, great! We'll have a feast tonight and tomorrow you can see Asira!"

Everyone got up and streamed out of the round house, but Lan stood frozen in place. Finally, he inhaled sharply and felt himself come back into one piece. Dazed, he looked around for Susie, but he was alone. Feeling empty and exhausted, he returned to his temporary house. What had just happened? Restlessly, Lan played over the events in the round house. This was not going how he had thought it would. Boosha had told him to deliver the keys and Empowerment to Asira. So where was she? He just wanted to finish his task and leave. Or maybe just leave. Looking around, he saw his cloak on the bed, but not his pack. The loss of his pack definitely stopped him from leaving.

Lan sat brooding. He'd escaped The Gatherers, made it through the Forest of Dandaka, and managed to get through the labyrinth by himself. Arriving at his destination was not supposed to be the hard part. And that Director! Lan felt nauseated thinking about him. He remembered what Sawyer had told him about the bioengineered species and how to recognize them through feelings of revulsion. Had humans been bioengineered, too?

But it wasn't just the Director that set Lan off. It was who he'd become when talking to Kuut. Back home, he'd never encountered anyone who made him naturally want to lie. He didn't even understand why he automatically tried not to tell the truth. It just felt like whatever he might have said was a bomb that would explode at any moment.

Finally, someone came to escort him to dinner. Lan briefly thought about wearing the cloak to look more imposing, but the weather was warm. The last thing he wanted to do was stand in front of the Director sweating profusely. Entering a smaller house than the communal one before, Lan tripped over the sill in the darkness. Flustered, he straightened, embarrassed at the thought of dozens of people witnessing his clumsy action. He was startled when he realized it was just Kuut sitting at a table, with one other servant off to the side.

"Come, sit down with me." Kuut gestured to the other end of the table. Lan walked over to the chair being held out for him by the servant, then felt his knees give out as the chair was pushed in. He collapsed heavily backward. This was getting worse by each minute.

"Try our special wine." Kuut acted like he hadn't noticed Lan's clumsiness and gestured to the servant. Like a bird hypnotized by a snake, Lan watched as a servant poured a lovely, amber liquid into a beautiful goblet to his right, then stepped back.

Lan hesitated. He'd never drunk anything alcoholic before. He'd watched as his friends in the village brewed their beer, but he didn't like the taste of it. As if reading his mind, Kuut exclaimed, "Oh, don't worry, it's not strong at all. Even your grandmother would approve of it."

Lan slowly picked up the goblet and brought it to his mouth. After his disastrous entrance, he didn't want to embarrass himself further by spilling a single drop. He took a small sip, hoping Kuut wouldn't notice how little he'd taken. His plan was to pretend to drink and to swallow as little as possible. He wasn't prepared for that tiny sip, though. The wine was the most delicious thing he'd ever tasted. It was buttery and fruity and popped a bit in his mouth before he swallowed. He couldn't help but take another sip, this time bigger than the last. Different flavors than before rolled across his tongue. Was that cucumber? Or maybe green apple? He had to try it again.

Vaguely he heard Kuut talking to him as the servants brought in their dinner. A fog seemed to descend over his mind that slowed down his responses. He thought he was saying very little in response to Kuut, but he was filled with picture-feelings with each of the Director's questions.

"Tell me about the Forest of Dandaka," Kuut asked. "Very few of us travel that way."

Lan thought he replied simply but in his mind the picture-feelings arose of the Map Compass and his journey through the forest. He saw and felt the arms of the Mother Tree and the joining together with the great white birches and all the others. He squinted across the room at Kuut. Was that the Map Compass by Kuut's side?

Feeling muddled, Lan instinctively grabbed the wine and took another sip. He looked down at his plate, still filled with food. He'd lost his appetite but he didn't want Kuut to know. He pushed some meat around on his plate and tried to make it connect with his fork.

Lan heard Kuut ask him something else, but he couldn't make out the words. New picture-feelings arose in him about Sawyer and making the bow, getting the rocks for the arrow tips, and then practicing shooting. As Lan was deep in the picture-feelings, remembering his time with Sawyer, he carefully tried to spear a piece of meat with his fork. He was really proud of himself when he nailed it after three tries, but then he missed his mouth and stabbed himself in the cheek. It struck him as extremely funny and he laughed out loud. Why had he been worrying about this dinner? This was so much fun!

Kuut murmured something else and Lan waggled his finger at him. He wasn't going to catch him out! But new picture-feelings started flowing through him. He was with Boosha and helping her when she was sick. Then she was handing him the Map Compass and the Crystal Cube. He heard her say, "Its name is Empowerment. Don't tell anyone its name."

At the other end of the table, something flashed in Kuut's hand. One part of Lan's brain wondered if the light came from his crystal, while another part of his brain pondered why Empowerment was flashing now when it hadn't before?

Before he could figure that out, more picture-feelings began pouring through Lan's mind. He saw The Gatherers chasing him across the field and hunting for him in the forest. As The Gatherers thundered through his mind, the room became still. It cut through the haze in Lan's mind and his vision began to clear. Then a loud crash rang through the room as Kuut sprang to his feet and his chair flew backward.

Lan heard him cry, "Get him out of here, now! He's going to bring The Gatherers down on us!"

Two men grabbed Lan by the arms and dragged him across the room. Lan's brain was still reeling with the effects of the wine as he tried to take in what was going on and get his legs underneath him. He stumbled as the men threw him into an open space. The fresh air and clear night sky steadied him and he lifted his face to locate the double moon. It had just risen behind the mountain in front of him and looked so normal compared to what was happening to him. An angry mob surrounded him, slowly closing in on him. He could hear their mutterings, "Crystalline! The Gatherers," but none of it made sense to him through the palpable hatred directed at him.

Someone struck him on the back and a sharp spike of pain arched through his body. In panic, Lan turned to face his attacker, but then someone punched him in the stomach and he doubled over, gasping for breath. He knew he had to stay upright and instinctively raised his arms to protect his head, but then crashed to the ground as more people attacked him. Lan felt each kick and punch until the pain rose fiery hot and consumed him like a forest in a raging fire.

From a distance Lan heard someone say, "Is he dead?" Lan's mind wondered the same thing. "Just about," he heard another person say. Then he heard the distinct voice of Kuut, "Throw him and his belongings in the midden. Let the birds and the wild animals take care of the rest. Do not mention him to anyone."

Lan floated in the air. Was he dead or was he being carried? He was beyond caring. One final moment of flying through the air, then Lan slammed onto something hard.

He sunk into the arms of the beckoning darkness and all pain stopped.

CHAPTER TWELVE

ESCAPE

Asira stopped to catch her breath while she scanned the skies. She hadn't seen or heard Sparky for a while. With the village a day behind her, she thought she'd feel either relieved to be gone or sad to leave her family. Instead, she felt jumpy. Even Takaani seemed unsettled. He kept stopping and looking behind him. When they started walking again, he whined and looked at her with sad eyes. In his picture language, he flashed her an image of Susie.

"I'm missing her, too," Asira told him. "Come on, we need to get to the foothills before dark."

Out of the corner of her eye, Asira saw a flash of red. Sparky swooped down and then did a few tight spirals in front of her. Asira couldn't move forward without bumping into him or Takaani. "Oh my Earth," she exclaimed, half annoyed and half laughing. "What is going on?"

Now Sparky sent images of Susie, too. Through his viewpoint, she saw Susie running up the path Asira had taken yesterday. She was carrying something blue.

Asira jogged up to a higher point and looked back down the trail.

The view from the top of the bluff was vast. Behind her and to her left was the imposing mountain Ausungate. Like a line someone had drawn in the dirt, she could see the river and beyond it the Forest of Dandaka. She couldn't see Our Place because it was tucked between the edge of the bluff and the river. Off to her right she saw the wild canyon land that marked the end of the seemingly quiet and placid river and the beginning of the wild, thunderous torrent leading to the waterfall. Asira had never heard a name for this land.

Far off in the distance, she saw a tiny figure. If she squinted she could make out a flash of blue but nothing else. The clear view was deceiving. Asira knew that the small figure was at least a half a day behind her.

"Is she thinking of coming with me?" Asira said aloud. That wouldn't work. Asira didn't want to go back ever and with Susie tagging along, she'd have to at some point. There was no answer from Takaani. The canine laid down, lifted his leg and started licking his butt. Sparky was also silent, spiraling up higher in the air, then taking off toward Susie. Maybe he would ask Susie what she was doing.

Asira sighed and sat down. Should she wait here for Susie, keep going and let her catch up, or trot back down and meet her half way? Either way she was going to lose time getting away from Our Place. Except she had already left Our Place. What was her hurry? Asira smiled at the urgency that was still driving her. Her parents had been gone for almost 12 years. One more day wasn't going to make much difference in her search for them.

Asira stood up and dusted off her traveling pants. They were a heavier material than the normal shift that she wore around Our Place. She wasn't used to the sound they made as she walked, but they were more practical for this journey. For one thing, with her hair tucked up under a simple hat, she didn't immediately stand out as a girl. She wasn't too worried about the dangers of the road for a young girl, though, with Takaani by her side.

Now she stood up and started hiking back toward Susie. Asira would lose half a day but if she could convince Susie to not follow her any further, the delay would be better in the long run. It was midafternoon before Asira met up with Susie. Her little sister's whole face lit up when she saw Asira standing in front of her.

Asira frowned and said sternly. "What are you doing? You shouldn't be following me."

"You have to come back," Susie said breathlessly.

"What? Why?" Asira turned and began walking back up the path toward the mountain. "Go back. Leave me alone."

"Stop, Asira. Look at this." Susie thrust out a blue cloak with geometric figures embroidered on it.

Turning, Asira felt disoriented to look at the cloak she'd seen in her vision. "Where did you get that? Has someone with that cloak come to the village and asked for me?" Worst timing ever, she told herself.

"Yes!" Susie said. "It was that boy I told you about. But now he's in trouble. Kuut had him beaten almost to death and thrown in the midden. I found this in his room." Again Susie held out the cloak.

Instinctively, Asira reached out to touch it, but then pulled her hand back. Nothing was changing her mind. "I'm not going back."

"You have to," Susie implored. "He came looking for you and now he's almost dead. He needs you to heal him."

Asira felt cold all over. This was exactly why she'd left. She knew visitors would be arriving soon now that the mountain passes were open. And that more people would come for healing. She couldn't do any more human healings. But then she remembered her fire vision and how she'd felt when she'd seen the figure in the blue cloak. She'd changed from being ready to end her life to choosing her own life and future. She felt torn apart with indecision. Part of her wanted to walk away, leave the village and all its troubles behind her, and part of her wanted to help this boy if he really was injured as badly as Susie said.

Sighing, Asira said, "You better tell me everything you know."

With those words, Susie knew Asira was going to come back to Our Place but just needed a last little bit of convincing. Using her most persuasive voice, Susie told her about Lan's arrival in the village and how he thought he was looking for a place named Asira and not a person. Then she told her of the dark mood of all the villagers and the meeting in the communal building, and how Lan said he'd been instructed to bring Asira something. Finally, Susie described the crystal Kuut had displayed for all to see.

How odd, Asira thought, thinking of her own crystal. "Then what happened?"

Susie said she watched Lan enter Kuut's house for dinner that night. She stayed, watching, until Kuut commanded his servants to throw Lan out into the square, yelling to everyone that he was a Crystalline and that The Gatherers were looking for him.

"I stopped watching when they began beating him." Susie's voice trembled and tears gathered in her eyes. Then she spoke in one rush of words. "I ran and got Dad. All he could do was follow them when they carried Lan to the midden and threw him in. When it was safe, Dad climbed down and found him. He carried him to your old place to recover, but Dad doesn't think he's going to make it. I snuck back to the room he stayed in to get his things, but all that was left was this cloak."

Susie paused to catch her breath. "You have to come back with me. Dad doesn't think he's going to make it without you. He says you need to come back."

Asira trusted her stepfather with every fiber of her being. He knew what it cost her to heal humans. If he said it was important, then it was important.

Turning home and starting down the trail, Asira sighed. She told herself this was only a slight delay in her plans. She'd take off as again as she soon as she could.

Lan watched with detachment as a man hovered over a body. He knew he should be concerned, but he wasn't. This wasn't like the time in Sawyer's hut when he'd been sucked down into the black hole with the scary things feeding off of him. Looking down, he realized he was seeing just a body. Maybe he'd become the hawk again like that time in his dreamy state.

The older man seemed very concerned for the body that lay so still. He heaped on blankets, Lan assumed to keep it warm. If the rest of the body looked like the bloodied, bruised, and gashed face and skull, that couldn't be good. It looked painful, but weirdly Lan felt no pain. In fact, he was extremely peaceful. He tried to tell the man it was okay, he was okay, but the man didn't seem to notice him as he hovered up by the ceiling.

A small girl entered the hut. The man looked up, relieved. "It may be too late. I can't get any response from him."

Behind the girl in the doorway stood a dog. It didn't look at the still figure lying on the bed but right up at Lan. That startled Lan. The dog could see him!

Out of the corner of his vision, he saw the girl place her hands on the body. He tumbled down from above into the sheer pain of his body. Lan was back in the village square. The agony of every kick and hit was intensified by the roar of the mob. The blows and the sounds mixed together until he couldn't tell if the screaming words being hurled at him or if the physical blows were what hurt the worst. He started to lift out of his body again, but the girl came to him and carried him away. The cessation of sound was so soothing.

He heard her speak again and again, "I am Asira. You must come back. You saved me once, now it is my turn."

Another time she spoke with impatience, "Why couldn't you

have worn the cloak? None of this would have happened."

Lan wasn't sure what she meant. He mulled over the words, but he couldn't really make sense of anything. He became aware of his heart and a deep hurt that had pierced it like a splinter. What had he done to these people to make them hate him so much and want him dead? He had come in good faith not knowing he had to protect himself. His village would have never attacked a visitor like this. He was asked to deliver a gift to someone in their town. Why was that worthy of hate? Why would anyone want to kill him over something like that?

Lan became feverish as he wrestled in his heart and soul about what had happened to him. At times, he was back in the square again trying to fight back. At times, he shouted at them to stop, that he had done nothing wrong. Each time the girl came and led him out of the mob. Slowly the splinter of their hate and his terror pulled out of his heart.

When the splinter of hate and fear lifted out almost completely, the energy of the Mother Tree rushed in, filling him with green vitality. Then he felt Boosha's love wash over him and the last of the splinter dissolved. He saw Boosha talking with the girl and wondered how they knew each other. Lan felt the girl's hands lift off of him and he rested in a deep, dreamless sleep.

Lan opened his eyes to silence. No, that wasn't correct. This was the silence created by the wind above the trees when no other sound was being made. The sound mixed with his breath. He felt like he was back in the Mother Tree. He turned his head slightly. In one corner sat a man on a low stool, slumped asleep against the rock wall. On the floor lay a girl who also looked like she might be asleep, but there was something about how she had positioned herself that didn't look like natural sleep. Next to her was a giant dog that Lan recognized as the one who'd seen him when he was floating by the ceiling. The dog watched the girl but waved his tail slightly when Lan took notice of him. With a start, Lan realized this was the dog who had also saved him in the labyrinth. He didn't know who the dog or the people were, but somehow he felt like he'd known them his whole life. After that disastrous beginning, he'd finally arrived where Boosha had told him to go.

Another small person burst into the hut. Lan recognized her as Susie, the little girl who'd followed him to his room when he'd first arrived in this village. "Dad! The Gatherers are coming."

The man in the corner leapt to his feet. He looked over at Lan and saw that he was awake. "Good. We have to go. I'm sorry you have to move so soon, but it is our only hope."

He bent down and shook Asira to wake her, but she didn't respond. He scooped her up and grabbed her pack. Takaani also stood up, shaking himself from head to toe, before following Susie, the man called Dad, and the inert form of Asira out the door. Lan sat up and slowly placed his feet on the ground. A wave of dizziness passed over him, his sight blackening almost completely. Susie came back and helped him stand up. She had his cloak over her arm. Together they moved out of the hut into the bright daylight. He stumbled as he was temporarily blinded by the sunlight. Susie steadied him and waited patiently for him to regain his balance.

Hesitantly, Lan began walking after the man he only knew by the name of Dad. Moving slowly, they walked away from the village and toward a mountain looming in the distance. Lan hoped they weren't trying to make it to the mountain, as it looked too far away for him to make it.

An hour passed and Lan made some small progress walking by himself. Asira lay in the man's arms, not moving but occasionally moaning. Lan wanted to ask what was wrong with her, but he needed his breath for every step he took.

They reached a big hole in the ground filled with strange items, all in some form of decay. Lan recognized some as metal, but couldn't identify them. He wondered if this is where the villagers found those items they sold in the market. The man gently placed Asira on the ground, then turned to Lan.

"This is where I found you," he motioned with his hand. "They threw your possessions in here, too. Let's see if we can find them. Susie, I want you to go back to your mother and if anyone asks where I am, tell them I'm checking traps for animals to sell. If they ask about your sister, tell them she left several days ago to hunt for herbs and that she'll be back soon."

Susie looked sad as she placed the blue cloak over Asira, and then with one last yearning look at Lan and her father, trotted back to the village. The man helped Lan over the lip of the hole, and then carried him on his back to a spot where Lan assumed he'd been found.

"What is this place?" he asked. "And why are you helping me?"

"Forgive me," the man said holding out his hand. Lan shook it weakly. "My name is Ryan. I'm father to Susie and Asira. This is the midden, a place left over from the time before the Great Shift. Have you never seen one before?" Lan shook his head.

"I'll tell you more about it later, but let's look for your things. What did your pack look like? And what was in it?"

A wave of longing washed over Lan for the familiarity of his pack and the precious contents. They represented his only connection to his life before arriving here. He disliked this town with every fiber of his being. Before, he knew people as generally good and generous, or obviously bad like The Gatherers. He'd never met people who seemed good on the outside but so mean and cruel on the inside. Other than Asira and her family, this whole village was full of people he never wanted to see again.

He weakly described his lost possessions as Ryan began looking through the discarded junk, "My pack was green. I had a Map Compass and a crystal in it. I also had a bow and quiver of arrows, some pine pitch sticks and a belt with my fire kit, a knife and a copper cup."

Ryan gave a triumphant but quiet shout and held up the pack. Looking inside, he grimaced at Lan. "Empty."

Lan couldn't breathe for a moment. How would he get back home without the Map Compass? And what was the point of coming, if he didn't have the crystal to give to Asira? If he ever saw Boosha again, he'd have to tell her he'd failed. Completely, colossally, epically. His mind went dark at the thought of disappointing Boosha or even worse. What if he never saw her again?

Seeing Lan's devastated expression, Ryan tried to reassure him while he continued to search. "They would have thrown away the Map Compass and the crystal. They wouldn't want to leave any sign of something that The Gatherers would associate with a Crystalline. Anyone who harbors a Crystalline bears the brunt of their wrath."

Lan opened his mouth to say he wasn't a Crystalline, but Ryan stopped him by holding up the Map Compass with a huge grin on his face. "Look!"

At the sight of the Map Compass, Lan exhaled suddenly, relief flooding his body all the way to his toes. Feeling stronger with hope, he stood up and began searching, too. After several minutes with no luck between them, Ryan said, "I've got an idea. Did your crystal have a name?" Lan nodded, wondering how he had known that.

"Say its name and let's see if anything happens."

Lan whispered, "Empowerment" and light shot from under a pile of refuse. Ryan raced over and dug it out. Picking it up gently, he placed it into the pack. He turned to Lan, knowing he was going to disappoint him with his next words. "I'm afraid the villagers probably kept your other things. And we need to get going to get a head start on The Gatherers."

Lan nodded numbly. His tools were a great loss to him. He knew he could probably make them all again, but they were the last connection to his friends and Boosha.

"I've got one last thing to do that might throw everyone off, if they do look for you," Ryan said. From his own pack, he removed some bloodied clothes that Lan recognized with a twist in his stomach as the ones he wore during the beating. Ryan began stuffing the clothes with grass, dirt and discarded items, then arranged them on the ground in the shape of a human body. At the top where the head should have been, he placed a round rock with some grass thrown over it. "If someone looks to see if you're still here, this might throw them off."

Lan moved slowly back to the edge of the midden. His foot tangled in something and he almost fell to his knees. Weakly, he reached down to detangle his foot and discovered his belt with his knife, cup and fire kit. His joy at recovering his belt gave him enough strength to climb over the lip of the midden. In silence, he and Ryan moved up the trail again, Asira in Ryan's arms and Takaani trotting beside them. They stopped later in the day in a small gully. Ryan told Lan to rest as much as he could, while he quickly set up camp and made a fire. He pulled out some food to heat and put on water to boil, adding some herbs to flavor it. As they sat eating, Lan looked over at Asira, still unconscious under his cloak. Finally, he asked, "What's wrong with her?"

"This is what happens to her after she works on humans," Ryan responded. "It can take her several days to come out of it. I don't know how long this time will last, though. She had to bring you back from the brink of death."

Lan was puzzled. "What do you mean, 'she works on humans'?"

Ryan looked at him over the rim of his cup of tea. He took his time answering, wondering how this young man could have been sent on a mission without any useful information. "She's a healer."

Lan took that in for several seconds, his head bowed over his plate. Looking up, his voice broke as he asked, "So I did this to her?"

Ryan shook his head. "This is just what happens to her. But she chose to come back and heal you."

Lan thought back to Boosha's urgent command to take Empowerment and the Three Keys to Asira. That was so long ago. Now, Asira, couldn't take Empowerment and he had no idea how to give her the Three Keys. He wondered if they would have helped her if he had given them to her. Tentatively he shared his thoughts with Ryan. "My grandmother told me to bring the crystal and the Three Keys to Asira."

Lan looked at Ryan out of the corner of his eye, wondering if he knew what the Three Keys were. Lan hesitated. Should he tell Ryan about The Gatherers that had come to his village? Afraid that Ryan would blame him for The Gatherers coming to Our Place, he didn't say anything. "My grandmother didn't tell me that Asira was a person or why I needed to bring her these things. I was too upset about leaving her to ask her because she wasn't feeling well."

Another wave of guilt passed over Lan. "My grandmother told me to wear the cloak when I arrived. But I didn't want to because it seemed too fancy." Looking at the cloak over the still body of Asira, that thought seemed ridiculous to him now. "Maybe all this wouldn't have happened."

Ryan shook his head. "You don't know what would have happened. And it's a waste of energy to wonder about it. Let's get some rest. It's imperative we reach the hidden recess tomorrow so I can get back to Our Place as quickly as possible."

CHAPTER THIRTEEN

NO TURNING BACK

Lan watched as Ryan strode down the hill. He had spent no time at the hidden dome. He made sure Asira was comfortable and warm and then prepared to return to Our Place. Lan was nervous to be alone with Asira. What if she didn't wake up? What if she did? Turning, he went back through the entrance of the dome.

Moodily he stared at Asira, lying on her side under the cloak. Takaani stretched out beside her, his giant head on his paws, his breathing synchronized with hers. He seemed to be waiting for something, perhaps some kind of movement. Ryan had left Lan with instructions for making a special herbal brew for Asira to keep her hydrated and nourished. After lifting her upright, Lan placed a cup to her lips. Asira opened her mouth and drank. It made Lan think she was faking this whole coma thing. He actually dropped her a bit, just to see if she would involuntarily yell out. When she didn't, Lan felt horrible for what he'd done.

When he wasn't watching Asira or pacing around the open-to-the-sky dome, he stared moodily at the Map Compass. It wasn't working again. Lan hoped it would help him find his way back to Boosha. Once Asira woke up, all he had to do was hand her the crystal and somehow give her the Three Keys, and he could go home. He wasn't sure how he'd get back if the Map Compass didn't help him, but he'd managed it once. How difficult could it be to reverse the path he'd followed? Lan resolutely chose not to think about his first disastrous days in the Forest of Dandaka, before he knew how to connect to the Golden Grid.

Several days passed. Occasionally, Takaani got up and left, then came back and laid down next to Asira again. Lan assumed he'd gone off hunting. He felt torn inside. Was he supposed to be doing something for Asira? He wondered if he could reach out to Boosha the way he had with the Mother Tree. Tentatively he sent his question to her through the Grid. "Boosha. I'm with Asira. She won't wake up. What should I do?"

He began to get images of himself healing the Badlands and receiving the initiations from Boosha. The memories flashed rapidly through his mind. Was he supposed to do the same for Asira? She was the healer, though, not him. Doing something, anything, felt less frustrating than sitting around doing nothing. He shied away from the thought that his actions might make her worse.

Lan took Empowerment out of his pack. Did he have to wear the cloak? It still covered Asira. He hadn't worn the cloak to heal the Badlands, so maybe he wouldn't need it now either. Standing, he began the Invocation to the Four Directions. Turning East, he raised Empowerment toward that direction and said the words that Sawyer had taught him, calling in the trees from the East and ending with "I choose to tell the truth without blame or judgment."

Slowly, he turned to each direction, making sure he said the words right. As he finished North with the words, "I choose to be open, not attached to outcome," his doubt fell away. He stood straight and tall as the birch trees. The trees were there in the dome, shimmering in the air, holding a container for himself and Asira for the next part. Takaani lifted his head off his paws and looked around. He felt or maybe saw the trees, too. Asira sighed but stayed in her deep sleep. Lan took heart because that small movement was more response than she given since they'd arrived at the dome.

Now, Lan gently touched Empowerment to her forehead and whispered, "May you honor the innate wisdom within all life." The crystal flashed in the quiet dome. Lan wasn't sure how long to wait. Was she going to heave and move like the land had done? Asira twitched slightly, her head moving from side to side, then she sighed loudly. Lan took that as a good sign and moved the crystal down to her heart. "May you remember, honor, and protect your gifts." The crystal flashed again. This time when Lan tried to move the crystal away, he couldn't. He stayed in that position for a long time, until Asira's chest rose up toward the sky and she sighed, and then sighed again. Lan moved the crystal to the place on her torso where her belly-button would be and stated, "May you become a Crystalline Expression of the Balance of All That Is."

After the iridescent flash from the crystal, Lan felt like someone pushed him back. Or maybe he fell back. At any rate, he was completely spent. Laying his head on the ground, Lan looked up and his breath caught. The open dome had filled with butterflies of every color and size. Takaani was jumping at them, trying to catch them in his mouth, but they were fluttering in spirals up and down, staying just out of his reach. As the last of the butterflies flew out of the dome, Lan heard Asira give a huge sigh. Lan smiled and then fell into his own deep, dreamless sleep.

The sunlight warmed Lan's face, then he smelled the fire and heard the sizzling of food cooking. Slowly he opened his eyes. Asira grinned at him from across the fire as she stirred something in a small pot. Her eyes were a brilliant, azure blue. He'd heard of the blue-eyed Crystallines but this was the first time he'd seen one. He was mesmerized.

"Hi," he said shyly. "How are you feeling?"

"I feel great!" Asira smiled warmly at him. "How are you feeling? The last time I saw you, you were rather beat up and not making much sense."

Lan laughed, relieved that Asira sounded like a normal person again. "I guess we both had a time of it for different reasons. Thank you for healing me."

"You're welcome," Then she spoiled the warm moment by adding, "You know, we could have avoided all that drama if you'd just worn the cloak."

Lan's eyes wavered and he busied himself putting on his shoes.

He mumbled, "I'm sorry."

Asira laughed. "Oh I'm just teasing you. Are you hungry? Here!" she handed him a plate of crumbled oatcake topped with berries. Lan gobbled it down. It was the best food he'd had for a long while.

He cleaned their plates and put away everything away in their packs.

As Asira stroked Takaani's head and back, she said to Lan softly, "Please tell me everything. Why were you looking for me? How did you get here? What did you do for me when I was in the coma?"

Lan opened his mouth, then shut it when his mind went blank. Where should he start? Should he tell her about the last few days when her father had brought them to this special hiding place? Or tell her about what had happened to him with Kuut before he got beat up and almost died? He decided to go all the way back to the beginning.

And so he began. He told her about Boosha being sick and calling him in to hand him the crystal and the Map Compass and telling him to go to Asira with the 3 Keys. He told her about The Gatherers, who had first taken his parents many years before, and how they chased him into the Forest of Dandaka. He told her about getting lost when he went into the black ravine and the pecan grove. Occasionally, Asira asked him to clarify something when he stumbled with his story, but mostly she remained quiet, listening deeply to every word.

Lan felt like he was telling her a story greater than just his words. At one point, she handed him a cup of water and he drank deeply, then picked up his story again.

Together they revisited his journey through the Forest of Dandaka, the meeting with the Mother Tree, and then dancing with the birches. He told her about the rough months when he'd run out of food and then went up to the hawthorn and got blasted. He introduced her to Sawyer and told her all that he had learned with him. Lan left out the part about his real name. It was too private. But then he told her about the Mammophants and the Day Out of Balance. Her eyes got big when he told her about the giant beasts. Next, he told her about the Three Keys and his initiation with the butterfly and the healing of the land.

Finally, he told her about arriving at the river. Asira smacked the ground with her hand. "I saw you!" she said. "That day you arrived at the river. I saw you but you weren't wearing the cloak, so I dismissed you as just another visitor coming for an animal or maybe a healing from me."

Lan stopped and asked her how she knew about the cloak. But Asira dismissed his question with a wave of her hand. "Finish your side of the story first."

Nodding, Lan told her about the maze under the river and how Takaani came and saved him. Asira hugged her steadfast companion, who wagged his tail. He gave a doggy smile with ears flattened back and his tongue hanging out. Asira marveled at how Takaani and Susie had known about this young man before she had.

Then Lan told her about all that had happened in the village and the dinner with Kuut. "He drugged you," Asira whispered in horror.

"That's how he got all that information out of you." She continued, "I saw the rest of that horrible night when I was healing you. Tell me what happened after I went into my coma."

Lan felt like he'd been talking for days, but it was only late afternoon. Though tired, he started telling the rest of what happened after she had healed him. His words slowed as he told about the trip to the midden, the flight to the hidden dome in the mountain and her father going back to Our Place to make sure Susie and Karen were okay. Finally, all that was left to tell was how he'd healed Asira. He told her how he had given her the Three Keys and used the Empowerment crystal. He described the moment the dome filled up with butterflies and how beautiful it had been.

"I wish I'd seen that," Asira whispered, this time in awe.

When he was done, Lan looked at her, filled with his own questions. "Let's eat and then I'll tell you my side of the story," Asira told him.

Lan felt as limp and empty as his torn clothes that they'd left in the midden. Their simple dinner revived him, along with the delicious tea Asira brewed. After cleaning up, they settled down next to a few still-glowing coals. Their shadows loomed on the granite stones around them while overhead the pine trees made black shapes against the deep blue twilight sky. The sound of the wind from high above was soothing, yet didn't touch them. It was Asira's turn to tell her tale.

Asira described her life in Our Place and the rise of her healing abilities. She talked about how her parents left and no one knew why or where they were, and her life with Ryan and Karen. Her face lit up when she talked about her healing work with the animals. Lan was intrigued by all of the animals around Our Place. They had so few back home. He wanted to ask her more questions about them but she shushed him and said, "Let's save the questions for later."

Lan sat in silence as her words and the picture-feelings flowed through him. She told him about Kuut wanting her to heal humans and how hard that was for her. Asira stopped for a moment and then told him, with a quiver in her voice, about her decision to end her life and how he'd appeared in her fire wearing the blue cloak. Somehow she knew he'd come to help her. Lan shifted uncomfortably when she shared that. He didn't feel like a hero to anyone.

As she talked about waiting for him, Lan compared his time line to hers. As she waited after her vision, he was recovering from the hawthorn sickness and then being tutored by Sawyer. Finally came that eventful day that Asira decided to not wait any more and leave Our Place.

When she finished her story, they both sat looking into the fire and not at each other. The moment had arrived when they had to figure out why they had been brought together. Lan was confused by some of the things she'd told him. How had he appeared in her fire? As for Asira, she didn't understand why he'd been sent to her, if he was just planning on turning around and going back to his grandmother. Without speaking their doubts and questions, they both retired to sleep. One thing they both felt—talking that much with someone else was exhausting.

In the morning, they looked at each other across the blackened coals of the fire, their eyes still full of questions. Asira held out her hand, "Can I see your crystal?"

Lan pulled his rucksack over and reached in. His voice was muffled as he pulled out Empowerment. "Here. I am supposed to give it to you."

Asira took it in her hands.

"Its name is Empowerment," he said. "Go ahead and say it."

When Asira said the name, nothing happened. It just sat in her hand. She handed it back to Lan. He wondered if it had broken when he used it with her.

"Empowerment?" he asked softly. Brilliant, iridescent light shot out of its center. Lan sighed with relief. It wasn't broken!

Asira took in the light with her endless blue eyes. "I think that one is yours," she said.

"But I was supposed to give it to you!" he exclaimed.

"Well, you did when you gave me the Three Keys. Look, I have my own." Now Asira pulled out her crystal from one of her bags. She held it up for Lan to see. It was infinitely more complex than Lan's simple cube crystal, with 20 sides of matching triangles.

"Does it have a name, too?" he asked her.

"Yes, it's called Crystalline Emotion." As Asira said the name, a beam of light shot out of its center. She gasped, "Oh! It's never done that before!"

Lan had a sudden hunch. "Asira, what color eyes do you have?"

"That's a silly question," she responded tartly. "You can see they are brown."

"No, Asira," Lan held her gaze steady with his own. "Your eyes are brilliant blue."

"But that's the color the Crystallines have," she exclaimed. "Kuut wouldn't have allowed me to stay if my eyes had been blue."

"Well, they're blue now," Lan said. "My own eyes changed color on my trip. They were brown before, too. Now they are amber. I think it happened because we both got the Three Keys."

Asira stood up and paced in agitation. "Are you The Awakener?" she asked.

"Am I The Awakener?" Lan suddenly connected the dots of the information that Boosha and Sawyer had given him. "I guess I am, but I don't think I'm the only one. Sawyer told me that all people used to have the Three Keys, but they went dormant during the Great Shift. Now only certain people have them. And those that have them can awaken them in other people."

"There were stories told in our town about someone called The Awakener. He or she was connected with the Crystallines. Kuut seemed to hate The Awakener as much as he hated the Crystallines."

"Do you think you are an Awakener now, too?" Lan asked.

"I hope not!" Asira shot back at him. "The last thing I need is to stand out even more than I do as a healer. And now you're telling me my eyes are blue, too!"

Asira and Lan sat in impasse. Lan was afraid to say anything because it might upset Asira more. Asira didn't want her carefully thought-out plan for her future to change.

"Back before all this happened to you and then to me, why do you think your Boosha sent you to me?" Asira asked.

"I don't know," Lan said miserably. "I just thought I had to deliver some things and then I could go back to my life. I'm hoping the Map Compass has started working again and I can go home." He reached into his pack and pulled out the Map Compass to check it. He didn't really expect much but it would be great if it was working again. He'd done what he'd been asked to do. Now it was time to go home.

Lan looked down at the Map Compass and froze. It worked! But it looked completely different than before. It still displayed the green square for the Forest of Dandaka, but now there was a new square, off to its right, with mountain peaks and the name Ausangate on it. In the upper corner were the names Asirali and Gavilan. The needle started there then swept in an arc to the lower corner, with the word Laird. "Umm, I don't think we're done with each other yet." Lan risked looking up at Asira. "Is your name by any chance Asirali?"

"How dare you! No one calls me that, ever!" Asira shot back. Silently Lan handed her the Map Compass. Asira looked at it with her face set in stone. "What is this?"

"I can't tell you," Lan responded. "All I know is that Boosha told me to go to Asira and that's how the Map Compass led me to you. Whenever I didn't follow its directions, I got into big trouble."

Lan flashed back to his vision when he received his 3rd Initiation. Softly as though not to startle a trapped animal, he asked, "Did you see or feel anything when I gave you the Three Keys?"

Asira hesitated. "The first one not so much. It felt like a wonderful wave of soft energy lifted me up."

Lan nodded. That was a good description for The Opening. "What about the second one?"

Asira's forehead crinkled as she frowned, trying to recall. "I don't know how to describe it. I looked into these blue eyes and felt like I had truly been seen all the way to my bones. I thought that was how it would be when I found my parents."

"Yes," Lan said, "That one is called The Chaos. Did you see anything with the third one?"

Asira opened her mouth, then stopped. Her face got the look that Lan was beginning to recognize as her stubborn side. "Nope, I didn't see a thing."

Lan decided to share his vision to see if she would let down her guard a bit. "I saw five people standing in a field looking at a city. One of those people was me and I was holding Empowerment in my hand. I didn't realize until now when you showed me your crystal, but one of those people was you. You were holding Crystalline Emotion. The other three had crystals, too. One was a girl who had wings, one was a guy with red hair, and one looked like neither a guy or a girl, but everyone had either bright blue or turquoise eyes. Except me. We were staring at this city and getting ready to go there."

Lan stopped to catch his breath. "I think we're supposed to travel together and meet each of these people. There's something we're supposed to do for The Balance of All That Is." As Lan spoke his thoughts out loud, he felt a wave of affirmation flow through him from Boosha, then the Mother Tree and then Sawyer. It was as if they were all standing around applauding him for figuring it out.

"Just you stop right now!" Asira jabbed her finger toward Lan's face as if that would make him stop talking. "I'm going to find my parents. I thought you were coming to help me. And then you told me that you were going back home and I was getting used to that idea, but now you're telling me that the two of us are supposed to go save the world or something!"

Lan didn't say it out loud but he thought "Yeah, and I thought I was the delivery boy and then I got to go home again."

Out loud he said, "Well, actually, the five of us."

"That's on you," Asira retorted. "What are you saving the world from?"

"I have no idea."

Asira snorted, "That's laughable, if it wasn't so sad. You're just trying to avoid going home and finding out that maybe Boosha didn't make it and she's dead."

Lan stood up, furious that she was taunting him. For a moment, doubt swept over him. Could she be right? He was avoiding going home because he was afraid to learn the truth about Boosha? Somehow having someone stand in front of him, putting his deepest fear into words, swept his doubt away. "This wasn't my plan for myself, either," he said in a low voice. "But I've been asked to do something and maybe it involves both of our parents and all the other Crystallines that have been taken, too. I don't have all the answers, but if there's one thing my journey has taught me, it's that something is guiding me and protecting me, so I'm going to trust that."

Asira was humbled by his words. But then she got mad again. He'd never had to put up with what she'd gone through. He was just a dumb, lucky boy. But she could use his help searching for her parents. Especially if her eyes had turned blue like he said.

She stuck out her hand to Lan and said, "Let's make a deal. We go and look for my parents first, then I'll help you find Laird."

Lan felt the weight of responsibility fall on him. How was he going to fulfill this task if he couldn't even get one person to believe him? He heard the despairing voice inside of him cry out silently, "I can't do it! Don't ask me."

Hoping he wouldn't regret it and not knowing what else to do, Lan slowly reached out and took Asira's hand, "Deal."

Enjoy a brief excerpt from Book Two of The Golden Spiral Series as Lan and Asira continue their journey through the sacred realms of Mt Ausangate in...

The Power of the Crystalline Horses

CHAPTER ONE

DAY OUT OF TIME

Draegan crossed the grounds from his mansion and approached the compound to check the different experiments being done on the Crystallines. Personally, he cared little whether Crystallines existed or not. But when the Illuminati returned, he wanted to show them he had completed the mission. Then perhaps he would be deemed worthy to go with them this time, instead of being left behind.

He entered the first compound and gazed through an observation window. Listless children sat around tables with art supplies, but very few sketched, colored or painted. One or two looked up with eyes that were cloudy and milky. Draegan signaled to the woman in charge, who came out to speak with him.

"How are they progressing?"

The large, matronly woman answered matter-of-factly. "These children over here have had eye worms now for more than a year. They are just about blind." She gestured toward another group of children. "These over here have had the worms for about six months. This is the phase when they are plagued with severe headaches." She waved her hand at another group off to the side. "These are the most recently infected. Their symptoms are mostly itchy eyes. We have to tie their hands at night to keep them from rubbing their eyes."

Draegan could see that all of them had listless spirits and yet still held tremendous amounts of light, except for the group that was almost blind. They looked as if their light had been, if not turned off, at least dimmed. They sat unmoving, interacting very little with anyone or anything. He wasn't sure if it was the children's eyes that made them Crystalline, but experimenting with their vision certainly was working at dimming their spirits.

Turning to the matron he said, "I want you to start giving them all the bleach drink. We need to speed up the process."

Draegan turned and strode to the next room. He watched at a window as scientists peered through special microscopes.

He pressed the button of an intercom and asked, "How are you doing with the gene splicing?"

One of the white-suited scientists stopped working and went to a similar intercom on the back wall. Pressing the button, he replied, "We have identified several gene factors that are unique to the Crystallines. We are experimenting with each one, implanting them in the children, to see which one turns off the special powers that they hold."

Draegan asked the most important question of all. "What is your timeline?"

"Six months to a year."

"Unacceptable!" Draegan snapped. "I want this done sooner. Report to me in three months with your progress." The scientist nodded in reply. He knew he couldn't explain to a nonscientist like Draegan why the process would take so long.

Draegan turned tensely and strode down to the third observation post. This was his social experiment. Here the children were subjected to hatred, playing a game of guards and prisoners. Before he could check in on the experiment, Tarek, his assistant, entered through a side door and came up to him.

As always, his hesitancy infuriated Draegan. "What is it? I'm assuming it's not good or you wouldn't be looking like a blind Crystalline."

"My lord," Tarek stammered. "We have heard from Occam Razor, the head of The Gatherers. They entered Our Place and searched it for any Crystallines or signs of Crystallines. The residents claimed they don't have any, nor have they seen any. Their director, Kuut, has always cooperated with us. What instructions should I give them?"

Draegan strode out of the building. The sky was overcast with an oppressive heaviness to it. He stopped and turned back to Tarek, scurrying to keep up behind him. "Is everyone accounted for in the town?"

"Only one person is missing. She's gone hunting for herbs."

"Well, who is this person?"

"She's a girl of about 13 years of age."

Draegan stiffened with those words. "Who is she? What does she look like?"

"According to Kuut, she's like the local healer. Her name is Asira. And she keeps the animals that they sell to those who come from the other regions." Tarek continued before Draegan could ask him what he knew he'd want to know. "She doesn't have the Crystalline eyes."

Draegan stomped down the path. He could feel the ripple of something out there that he didn't like. The energies were gathering and he couldn't put his finger on what was happening or where it was coming from. "Anything else?"

"There was one irregularity. This town has a midden from before The Shift. Occam Razor had The Gatherers search it and they found clothes that were covered with blood. No one claims to know anything about them." Tarek prayed he wouldn't be another victim of "kill the messenger" syndrome.

"That's it. We're done playing this the gentle way." Draegan snarled. "I want whoever tripped that tree glyph found and found now. Isn't there an ancient maze near that town?"

Tarek was surprised that Draegan remembered the maze. "I believe there is."

"You tell Occam to take Kuut and throw him in and block up the entrance. Then go and ask the next resident about those clothes."

Tarek nodded, glad to be done with the uncomfortable conversation. He ran off to the communication room to prepare the message for sending. If those villagers didn't cooperate, the wrath of Draegan would be on their heads.

Lan woke with a start. He saw Asira standing on a rock above him with Takaani by her side. She was looking down at him and laughing. Suddenly, he felt his skin crawling. Glancing down he saw he was covered in crickets slowly marching across his body. They seemed to be munching on his clothes as they went.

With a shout, Lan leaped up. "Why didn't you wake me?" he yelled to Asira as he brushed the mostly harmless insects off of him. His clothes were now filled with holes. Looking behind him the ground was covered with slow moving crickets eating as they marched. Grabbing up his gear, then jumping from rock to rock, he made it over to Asira's rock and climbed up.

"It's the Day Out of Time, isn't it?" he asked her. Lan didn't need her answer. He was annoyed he'd missed the signs leading up to this day. He'd been so focused on his annoyance and irritation with Asira that he was disconnected from everything.

This journey was beyond frustrating. Asira thought she was the boss of every decision and wouldn't listen to him. Lan liked to talk out their decisions and come to a consensus but that was too slow for Asira. She took action first and then thought about it later. Lan couldn't remember the last time he'd felt connected to the Golden Grid.

The last of the crickets passed. Lan gloomily watched the last ones eating the ones in front of them because there was nothing left to eat. He stared in horror at their campsite. He'd forgotten his shoes in his dash to get out of the way and now just a few pieces were left.

"That's it for me," he said. "I quit."

An Important Afterword

Did you like the story of Lan and Asira? Please leave a comment on Amazon about it so other Crystallines can find it.

And get more great back material about the book such as the sounds that trees make, the Tree Calendar, invocations and more all at http://thegoldenspiralseries.com.

Sign up for the newsletter and get advanced notification about the unfolding of the next book in the series.

Parents, do you have Crystalline children? Learn how to work with their energy with the Three Keys and sacred geometry shapes at http://ccthealing.com

ABOUT THE AUTHOR

g.c. Ramirez is an awesome navigator of all things energy. She grew up on a ranch in Montana where the trees and horses were her daily friends and taught her how to read energy.

As an adult, she pursued energy healing and went on to create her own modality called Crystalline Consciousness Technique™. gia has written many manuals and nonfiction books for her classes and programs.

A couple of years ago, gia got a picture-feeling that would not leave her. It was the opening scene of *The Power of the Crystalline Trees* with Lan and Boosha in their cottage. She knew she needed to tell the story of the Crystallines and the Golden Spiral. Her life has never been the same.

gia still lives on her family ranch in Montana where she holds programs and classes for Crystalline Kids (of all ages). She's currently working on a card deck for role-playing in the Golden Spiral Series and book two in the series.

www.ingramcontent.com/pod-product-compliance
Lightning Source LLC
Chambersburg PA
CBHW032212190626
46810CB00019B/2660